"I was your wife."

Aidan's eyes narrowed to slits. "*Was* being the operative word."

Her heart pounded so hard, Yvonne was sure he could see it fluttering the ruffles on her shirt. "*Wife* being the important one. I just want to make sure we can work together."

"You really don't know why my mother hired you, do you?"

Suddenly uneasy, she kept any hint of it out of her tone as she said, "She hired me to plan her wedding. And because the Diamond Dust needs someone to help coordinate events."

"First of all, we only decided to start hosting events Sunday night—and before you start counting, that was only three days ago. And, out of all the events coordinators in the South, she hired you. It never occurred to you to wonder why?"

Yvonne brushed a piece of dog hair off her skirt. "She needed someone with experience. Someone willing to relocate—"

"She hired you," he said flatly, "because she thinks if we work together, if you're back in Jewell, you'll get back in my life. She hired you because she wants us to get back together."

Dear Reader,

I firmly believe in second chances. Maybe that's why I love reunion stories so much. Going along on the journey with two people who've drifted apart only to find their way together again always leaves me with a smile and a sense of closure—it's as if things have finally turned out the way they were meant to.

That's how I feel about *Feels Like Home*. Though Aidan and Yvonne have been divorced for many years, they were meant to be together. Unfortunately, bringing them back together wasn't as easy as I'd hoped!

If you've read either *A Marine for Christmas* or *The Prodigal Son* you know Aidan is stubborn, bossy and a bit arrogant. So, of course, getting him to realize he'd made his fair share of mistakes during his short-lived marriage wasn't easy. But it was so worth it.

I try to make sure my characters earn their happy ending, that they grow and change as a result of the conflicts in the story. But mostly, I want them to become their best selves by loving, and receiving love from, the person they were meant to be with.

Though both Aidan and Yvonne have changed since she walked out on him years ago, the past is right there, between them every step of the way. Only when they're able to see the other in the present, only when they're able to forgive, can they move on to the future.

I can't believe it's time to say goodbye to The Diamond Dust and the Sheppards. I had a great time getting to know these characters and writing their stories, and I hope you enjoyed reading them, as well.

I love to hear from readers. Please visit my website, www.bethandrews.net, or write to me at P.O. Box 714, Bradford, PA 16701.

Beth Andrews

Feels Like Home
Beth Andrews

TORONTO NEW YORK LONDON
AMSTERDAM PARIS SYDNEY HAMBURG
STOCKHOLM ATHENS TOKYO MILAN MADRID
PRAGUE WARSAW BUDAPEST AUCKLAND

Recycling programs
for this product may
not exist in your area.

ISBN-13: 978-0-373-71727-9

FEELS LIKE HOME

ABOUT THE AUTHOR

Romance Writers of America RITA® Award Winner Beth Andrews lives in Northwestern Pennsylvania with her husband and two teenage daughters. During the course of writing her Diamond Dust trilogy, she purchased copious amounts of wine, purely for research purposes. When not drinking...er...*researching* she can be found in the passenger seat of her SUV gripping the dashboard, slamming her foot on a nonexistent brake and praying fervently. Or, in other words, teaching her older daughter to drive. She still counts the days until her son returns from college—mainly because he already knows how to drive. Learn more about Beth and her books by visiting her website, www.BethAndrews.net.

Books by Beth Andrews

HARLEQUIN SUPERROMANCE

This book is dedicated to all whose lives have been touched by cancer. And to the men and women who devote their lives to finding a cure.

Acknowledgments

My sincere gratitude to Mitzi Batterson of James River Cellars Winery in Glen Allen, VA.

CHAPTER ONE

OH, DEAR LORD, what had she gotten herself into?

A cool breeze blew Yvonne Delisle's hair into her eyes and she impatiently tucked it behind her ear as she stared up at the ancient carriage house. Her career as a wedding consultant, the sixteen years she'd spent on the pageant circuit and, most importantly, being the only child of Savannah social royalty Richard and Elaine Delisle, had all taught her one very important fact.

Appearances counted.

Especially when it came to weddings. So why on earth retired senator Allen Wallace and vineyard owner Diane Sheppard would want to have theirs in this particular building was beyond her. The wood siding was weathered and mottled, ranging from a dull gray to deep tan. Shingles were sliding off the steeply pitched roof. What glass was left in the windows was scratched beyond repair, and the left side of the overhang above the double carriage doors dropped precariously.

She tucked her cold fingers into the short pockets of her fitted jacket. Then again, it wasn't up to her to decide where her couples got married. If it was, the Shields-Larson wedding never would've taken place at a dairy farm—complete with mooing cows and the pungent smell of manure.

No, she thought as she crossed to the building's wooden door, the tall heels of her black pumps wobbling on the gravel drive. Her job was to make sure the bride got exactly what she wanted. Whether the wedding took place at a church, the beach or a carriage house that looked as if it should be condemned.

She hoped it didn't fall down while she was inside.

With a quick prayer, she unlocked the door and stepped in. The smell hit her first—wet wood, motor oil and dust. Then she realized that even though the morning sunlight filtered through the dirty windows, it was colder inside than out. Leaving the door open, she flipped on the light switches. Several bare bulbs hanging from low-lying rafters flickered to life.

At least it was big enough to accommodate several hundred guests. Or it would be once it was cleared out. The place was packed with cardboard boxes, plastic tubs, shovels, rakes and other implements, wine barrels ranging from short and squat to one that reached her shoulder, old tools and large glass jars on a three-tiered wooden shelf.

Eyes narrowed, she turned in a slow circle and imagined the space as it could be. It had high ceilings, wide-planked floors and two exposed-brick walls. With some cleaning—okay, a lot of cleaning—a few coats of paint and new windows, it could be charming. In a rustic sort of way.

Maybe, just maybe, this could work.

She dug her BlackBerry from her purse and started to pace, kicking up dust as she typed in notes.

Candles. Dozens and dozens of white candles of all shapes and sizes. Miniature white lights strung along the rafters. Turning, she walked back to the door. She wasn't due to meet with Diane until this afternoon, so didn't know if the woman had already chosen a color scheme or not, but Yvonne was thinking chocolate-brown and bright green. Or better yet, brown and robin's egg blue.

She could incorporate the wine barrels into the decor. Use corks as name card holders. This wasn't just the setting of Diane Sheppard's second wedding after all; the Diamond Dust was her winery. A huge part of her life. Yvonne put her phone away, hung her purse on the handlebars of a faded red Huffy bike and set out to see what else she could find of use.

Twenty minutes later she'd accumulated several glass bottles, a wooden shutter she had no idea how she'd ever use but hadn't been able to pass up and some wide picture frames. And then she saw it. The inspiration for the head table's centerpiece—an antique lantern.

Now all she had to do was get to it. Easier said than done, as it was on top of some sort of workbench behind at least three feet of junk. Grabbing the arms of a hideous velvet high-backed chair, she pulled. Nothing happened. Not only was this the ugliest chair she'd ever had the misfortune of seeing, it was also the heaviest.

She slid her snug skirt up a few inches, bent and adjusted her grip on the chair.

"Excuse me." She froze. That deep, oh-so-familiar voice. A voice that, even after all these years of trying to get him out of her head, Yvonne still heard in her dreams. "What the hell do you think you're doing?"

The nape of her neck prickled. She didn't have to turn to know that Aidan Sheppard stood behind her, getting a good look at her rear. She straightened quickly, swayed a little before regaining her balance.

"Hello, Aidan," she said, praying he didn't notice the slight tremor in her voice. She smoothed her skirt back down to just above her knees, then turned. "How are you?"

He looked older, of course. She'd expected that. What she hadn't expected was her reaction to him. Her mixed emotions. He was so tall and lean and…male. Unshaven, his face was sharper, the angles more pronounced. His shoulders broader in his sweaty, white T-shirt.

But his eyes were the same, a light blue with enough green in them to make it seem as if they were ever changing. For so long, she'd tried to be the woman he saw with those eyes. Until she realized she'd much rather be loved for herself.

"What are you doing here?" he repeated.

"I was trying to move this." She indicated the chair. "I saw that lantern and—"

"And you thought you'd take it?"

She pursed her lips. "To use as a centerpiece," she clarified.

He looked pointedly at the other items she'd collected. "And you couldn't find a lantern—or any of this other stuff—in Charleston?"

"I'm sure I could. But I'm not in Charleston, am I?"

"Which brings me back to my original question."

"I wanted to check out the building, see what I have to work…" His words sank in. She frowned. "What do you mean?"

He raised one eyebrow. "What are you doing in Jewell? Why are you on my family's property?"

Surely Diane—Mrs. Sheppard—wouldn't keep something this…big, important, awkward…from her son. Would she? "Didn't your mother tell you?"

"Obviously not."

Yvonne forced herself not to stare at his bare legs. He must be getting cold in those running shorts. "She hired me."

Thanks to her parents' tutelage in presenting an unruffled facade in any given situation, there was no way he could sense her nervousness. Her uncertainty.

"To work at the Diamond Dust," she added when he said nothing.

"Is that so?" he murmured. "In what capacity?"

"She… I…" Yvonne licked her suddenly dry lips. She tugged at the bottom of her jacket. "I'm an events coordinator."

He just stared.

Maybe her mother had been right and this was a mistake. A huge one. Maybe Yvonne shouldn't have come here.

Shouldn't have thought—hoped—Aidan would forgive her.

"You're an events coordinator," he said. It wasn't a question.

"Yes. My specialty is weddings."

"Weddings," he repeated in a monotone. "Putting that business degree to good use, I see."

Ducking her head so he couldn't see that his dig had hit home, she shoved the chair a few more inches to get behind it. His was a familiar set-down, one she'd heard often enough from her parents. One she knew better than to respond to.

"Yes, well, plans change," she said, moving aside a box of record albums. "But you already know that, don't you?"

As soon as the words left her mouth, she cringed. She wasn't here to antagonize him. She was here to do a job.

But Aidan he didn't seem angry that she'd reminded him of his own forgotten plans. In fact, he now seemed indifferent...to the cold *and* to her.

She wanted to throw her shoe at him. Or that damn lantern. If she ever reached it.

"Since you seem surprised to find out your mother hired me," Yvonne said, setting a tarnished brass table lamp on the chair, "I suppose she also didn't mention that I'll be staying here, as well."

"Tell me you mean *here* as in the town of Jewell."

"At the cottage. It seemed more…convenient…than trying to find a place in town."

"We wouldn't want you to be inconvenienced now, would we?"

"I offered to pay rent," she assured him. "But your mother said it was empty, and included lodging as part of my fee." She met his eyes unflinchingly. "I wouldn't want you to think I'm taking advantage of Diane's generosity."

"One thing I never worry about is my mother being taken advantage of."

Yvonne would have smiled, if he wasn't looking at her so coldly. "No. Of course not. Diane's very…capable." Capable. Confident. Intimidating. Almost as intimidating as her own mother.

Yvonne leaned against the hard edge of the counter and reached for the lantern. Her fingertips grazed the metal base. She glanced over her shoulder at him. "I don't suppose you could…?"

"No."

His refusal surprised her. He'd never refused her anything before. But that was then, she reminded herself.

She searched the area and spied a blue metal toolbox halfway under the bench. Kneeling, she wrestled it forward. "Do you…are you living here as well?" she asked, straightening. "At the Diamond Dust, I mean."

Generations of Sheppards had lived at the historic plantation.

Aidan didn't jump in to tease her out of her nerves. Smooth things over. He simply crossed his arms. "No."

He certainly was getting good at using that one word with her. *How was he not freezing in his running gear?*

She turned her back to him and quickly pulled her skirt halfway up her thighs. Her face was so hot, she expected her hair to catch on fire. She stepped onto the toolbox, grabbed the lantern and stepped back down.

And yanked her skirt back into place.

"So you're still at the house?" she asked, the lantern clutched to her chest.

The bungalow with vaulted ceilings and bright, airy rooms.

Their house.

"What I can't help but wonder," he said, "is what made you or my mother think that you working here would be a good idea."

"I can't speak for your mother..." Even if she could, she wouldn't dare. "But I wanted a change. A challenge."

And God knew getting the carriage house ready for a wedding in just over a month certainly qualified.

"Got tired of hosting fundraisers and attending luncheons at the country club?" he asked, as if they were discussing nothing more important—or interesting— than a round of golf.

Her grip on the lantern tightened. The corner of it

dug into her ribs. He'd always treated her as if she was delicate. Someone best suited to look pretty on his arm. To be charming and sweet, and agree with him. To stand back and let him handle everything.

As her parents had taught her.

Just, she could admit—if only to herself—as she'd let him believe.

But she wasn't that person anymore.

"Actually," she said, "I've been working for World Class Weddings for the past five years." And from the blank look he gave her, he had no idea what she was talking about. "It's a wedding planning service in Charleston. One of the best."

The sun streamed through the doorway, haloing Aidan in soft light. "And you decided to give that up to come work here?"

"I'm not giving anything up." Which was one of the reasons she'd ultimately decided to accept Diane's offer. "I'm excited to be here. To help build the special events side of your business from the start." And then she'd go back to her job, back to her friends in Charleston.

"Unfortunately," Aidan said—how she hated his sarcasm— "I don't share your enthusiasm."

"My enthusiasm for...?"

"Any of it." His T-shirt pulled snug against his shoulders as his hands fisted beneath his crossed arms. "The winery hosting events, and mainly, you being anywhere near my family's business."

Though she told herself his opinions, his likes and

dislikes, didn't matter to her, not anymore, she was disappointed. "Oh. Well, maybe in time—"

"Time isn't going to change my mind. And even if it could, it wouldn't matter, because you won't be here."

"I don't understand."

"Let me make it clear to you, then," he said flatly. "You're fired."

YVONNE BLINKED. Blinked again. But when she spoke, her voice was as precise, as unfailingly polite, as always. "You can't fire me."

Aidan wanted to throw that damn chair through a window. "I can't?" He smiled.

She hesitated, confusion clouding her brown eyes. "No. I have a contract."

"A contract with the Diamond Dust?"

"Of course." Yvonne tilted her head so that her blond hair fell over her shoulder. He didn't doubt the move was practiced. Just as rehearsed as her placid expression and condescending tone. "Would you care to see it?"

Though his mother owned the business, Aidan was the one in charge. All contracts went through him first. Everything to do with what he still called his father's winery—which, in a matter of months, would be *his* winery—went through Aidan first. "I can't think of anything I'd like more." Except throwing her off his property for good.

"I left it in my car," she said. She looked at him uncertainly. "If you'll excuse me?"

And that's when he realized she wasn't being polite. She wanted him to move.

With a mocking bow, he took a deliberate step to the left, giving her plenty of space. "By all means. The last thing I'd want is to get in your way. Not when you have your heart set on leaving."

Her step faltered. But then she continued on, her gait measured in her tight skirt. The sound of her high heels faded as she walked out the door.

But unlike her exit seven years ago, this time he was the one in control.

He followed her outside and watched as she crossed to her silver Lexus LS. She moved like the debutante she'd been—the sway of her hips subtle, her slim shoulders back. He watched as she slowly crossed the gravel driveway and opened her car door before sitting in the driver's seat.

She was, as always, cool. Reserved.

Beautiful.

It'd been that beauty and her air of *you can't touch this* that'd drawn him to her in the first place.

And he married her—loved her—despite her aloofness. He'd wanted to have children with her, have a life with her. Grow old with her.

But she'd left. And she had no right to come back.

The sweat had long since dried and cooled on his body as he stared over the car to the rolling hills surrounding his family's property. Hard to believe not fifteen minutes ago it'd been just a normal Wednesday morning run. And then he'd reached the carriage house and discovered Yvonne digging through his father's junk in that damn skirt and a short, snug jacket that emphasized her tiny waist.

He smirked. Once a beauty queen, always a beauty queen. Even in dust, grime and rodent droppings.

Yvonne climbed out of the car with a large manila envelope in her hand. By the time she reached him, his expression was once again carefully neutral, his shoulder relaxed.

She held out the envelope. "See for yourself."

Aidan took it, not letting their fingers touch. He flipped it over. The shipping label was addressed to World Class Weddings, care of Ms. Yvonne Delisle.

She hadn't kept his name.

He pulled out the sheaf of papers inside and quickly scanned them.

"Looks like a standard contract," he said, forcing his tone to remain impassive. "Nothing that can't be voided."

She inhaled sharply. "I'll sue."

He almost laughed. "Drag your company, your family's name, through the legal system?" Wouldn't her father love that? And God knew, Yvonne didn't do anything without her parents' approval. "I don't think so."

"Don't underestimate me, Aidan," she said softly.

His blood heated. Underestimate her? He'd loved her. Given her everything he had.

"Don't push me," he warned gruffly. "I'm not one of those nice Southern boys your daddy handpicked for you."

Although if she'd stuck with one of those pasty-faced men with old money and "the third" after their names, men who spent their days working for their fathers, their evenings at the club and their weekends with their mistresses, he'd have been better off.

"I'll have to take my chances then," she said.

"Why?"

After a moment, she shrugged. "I want this job."

"And what daddy's little princess wants, she gets. Isn't that how it goes?"

"If it makes you feel better to believe that, go ahead."

"You don't know how much that means to me. Your permission."

"Aidan, please," she said, her voice washing over his cool skin like a warm shower, "I realize this came as a surprise to you, and I don't know why your mother didn't tell you about our agreement, but I was hoping we could get past our history." She looked up at him from beneath her dark lashes. "I know it'll be…awkward… at first and I realize you're still angry with me—"

"I'm not," he lied smoothly. A lie he wanted to believe. Because to be angry meant he still felt something for her.

Relieved, and she smiled as she laid her hand on his forearm. His breath lodged painfully in his lungs. His muscles tensed under her soft fingers. But he didn't shake her off.

"Then you shouldn't have any objection to me working at the Diamond Dust," she said.

"I'm not angry," he repeated and, slowly deliberately, removed her hand from his arm. "But I still don't want you here."

She sent him a pitying look, setting his teeth on edge. *She* pitied *him?*

Damn it all to hell. Damn her to hell.

"And what Aidan Sheppard wants, he gets," she said, tossing his words back at him.

That wasn't true. And that was okay. He understood life wasn't fair. Didn't expect it to be. But this time, this one time, he deserved to get exactly what he wanted.

"You'll be well compensated for your time and travel expenses," he said, sliding the contract back into the envelope and handing it to her. "Be off my family's property by five and we'll pretend this never happened."

Before he'd even finished speaking, she started shaking her head. "This—" she waved the envelope "—states I'm employed for the next six weeks."

He tapped his fist against the side of his thigh. She'd never been stubborn before. Had always compromised. Or, in most cases, gave in.

"What do you want?" he asked.

"I want those six weeks."

"Why?"

She frowned. "I told you, I—"

"I know. You want this job. But why here? Surely there are other opportunities out there far away from Jewell."

"The first wedding here will be your mother's."

"My mother's wedding isn't until July."

Yvonne shook her head. "Diane said she and the senator were moving the date up to April 9."

And the surprises just kept piling up. He hated surprises.

"You're going to be in charge of planning my mom's wedding? Of course you are," he said before she could respond. "What wedding planner wouldn't want to be in charge of possibly the most talked about event of the year so far? After all, Al's a beloved ex-politician. A wealthy ex-politician with powerful connections. And if the wedding is deemed a success, well, then who gets the credit?" He watched her carefully. "You do."

Two spots of color appeared high on Yvonne's cheeks. "It's not about taking credit."

"No. It's about you using my mom's wedding as a way to help your career. Sorry, Princess, but I'm not about to let that happen."

At the use of his old nickname for her, she blanched. "You don't have a say. I went into this contract with Diane, and unless she terminates it, I'm staying."

You don't have a say.

Just as he hadn't had a say about the end of their marriage. Resentment churned in his stomach. But he didn't give in to it. He walked away. Because no one made Aidan Sheppard lose control. Especially not Yvonne *Delisle.*

CHAPTER TWO

"WERE YOU GOING TO TELL me?" Aidan asked as he entered his mother's spacious kitchen. "Or was I suppose to find out myself?"

Pouring coffee into a mug, Diane Sheppard glanced at her son. Even when he planned on working out in the vineyards all day, he looked as if he'd stepped out of some sort of catalog. He had on loose cargos and a plaid denim work shirt open over a waffle knit Henley. His short hair was neatly combed, the golden strands dark and damp from a recent shower.

As usual, Aidan had arrived at the break of day for a run around the vineyard before returning to shower and dress in the bathroom adjoining his office upstairs. All before she'd even had her cup of coffee.

Her eldest loved nothing more than his routine, his schedules and his family.

It was up to her to help him see there was more to life than the first two. That he didn't have to sacrifice so much for the third.

"I'm afraid I can't answer that, as I have no idea what you're talking about." Although she could guess.

Diane sighed. This conversation was not going to be easy.

She tightened the sash of the new knee-length, velour robe she wore over her pajamas. Then again, no one ever said doing the right thing was easy.

"Coffee?" she asked.

Not waiting for an answer, she poured him a cup.

He accepted it without taking his eyes off her. "I'm talking about you hiring my ex-wife to work at the Diamond Dust."

He watched her steadily, his eyes a cross between her own blue ones and the green of his father's. But under his careful detachment, she sensed his agitation. His anger.

Her sons. Though they tried, they couldn't hide anything from their mother.

"I was going to tell you," she said, adding cream to her coffee before crossing to the large, granite-topped island to sit on one of the high-backed stools, "when I deemed the time right."

His jaw worked—throwing away all the money she'd invested in his orthodontic care as a teen by grinding his teeth to dust. "I'd say the right time is now. Seeing as how I discovered Yvonne picking through Dad's stuff at the carriage house while I was on my run."

"Oh?" Diane sipped her coffee to hide her surprise. "I wasn't expecting her until this afternoon."

She'd last spoken to her the night before, when Yvonne had called to let Diane know she'd received the signed contract and the keys to both the cottage and the carriage house. Diane had half thought Yvonne wouldn't show up at all. Returning to Jewell couldn't be easy for the younger woman. Not after how things ended between her and Aidan. How she'd ended things between them.

And though Diane had nothing against her ex-daughter-in-law, Yvonne had never struck her as being brave enough, strong enough or self-sufficient enough to tackle the difficult things in life head-on.

Lord knew, Aidan could be all sorts of difficult.

But she'd hoped the promise of a new contract would bring her back. Good to know she'd been right. Again.

"What the hell were you thinking?" Aidan asked.

She narrowed her eyes. But since his reaction—and his insolent tone—were quite understandable, she took another drink instead of calling him on it. "I was thinking that she'd be the best person to plan my wedding."

"Your wedding. Right," he said. "Would this be the wedding you've moved up by three months without telling your family?"

"I—"

He held up a hand. "Wait. Let me guess. You were going to tell us. When you deemed the time right."

"I was going to tell you," she said frostily, "at lunch tomorrow. After a few more details had been nailed down."

"Why move it up at all?"

"Yvonne's already booked for the summer and this

was the only time her company was willing to spare her for a few months." What she didn't mention was the exorbitant fee she'd agreed to in order to get World Class Weddings to let their most popular planner leave for six weeks. "Al and I moved the date up so she could take the job." She smiled brightly, as if Aidan wasn't trying to skewer her with his glare. "From all accounts, she's one of the best wedding planners in the South."

Her stubborn son seemed less than impressed. "And since you hired her to plan your wedding, you decided to throw in a job at the winery as a bonus?"

"I decided that we could use someone with her skills and connections to help get our events business off the ground."

"Get off the ground? We decided only three days ago to start hosting events. I thought we'd do a little research. See if this idea is even feasible before committing to it."

"We're already committed. You and your brothers agreed—"

"They agreed. I just went along with the majority vote."

As if she didn't realize how much that had bothered him—no longer having sole authority over all decisions made at the winery. Oh, she was still the owner, but for the past eight years, Aidan had run the company with little input from her. Once he and his brothers became full partners in July, when she retired, that would all change.

"It's a done deal," she said. "Which was why I wanted to get the ball rolling. I see no sense in putting this off."

He stared at her as if he could look inside her head and sort through her lies. "You haven't had more than a passing interest in the company since Dad died. Why get involved now?"

Guilt squeezed the air from her lungs and she stared blindly at the rings on her right hand. The rings her first husband had given her. The rings that, despite being engaged to another man, despite being in love with Al, she hadn't been able to take off.

What Aidan said was true. So true. When she'd lost Tom, she'd stopped caring about the Diamond Dust. They'd started the winery from the ground up—literally. They'd planted the vines. Nurtured them and helped them grown. They'd renovated the original farmhouse into the gift shop-tasting room with their own hammers and nails, had come up with a business plan, taught themselves how to run a successful winery.

But without her husband by her side, she hadn't wanted anything to do with the business they'd built together. So she'd turned to Aidan, who'd given up his own ambitions to keep his father's dreams alive.

And she'd let him.

"Though I may have taken a...backseat at the winery these past few years," she said, wrapping her fingers around the base of her mug. "I'm always interested in what's going on with my company."

"Funny how your interest just happens to involve my ex-wife."

"We need her. Connie doesn't know how to get the winery ready, so I hired Yvonne as a consultant."

Their vineyard manager, Connie Henkel, had been a valuable employee ever since she'd started working there sixteen years ago. But now that Diane's youngest son Matt—a noted vintner who'd worked at some of the best wineries in the world—had agreed to join the winery a few weeks ago, Connie had been forced to share her duties with him.

"There's no way Connie can tackle this job on her own," Diane continued. "Besides, with her helping Matt manage the vineyards, her time is limited."

"There's no need for her to help Matt," Aidan said as he refreshed his coffee. "He's more than capable of running things on his own."

"Keeping Connie from those vineyards is like trying to stop the rain from falling. She loves them."

"Then I guess you should've thought of that before you blackmailed Matt into joining the company."

"I did," she said, regret making her voice sharp.

Of course she'd thought of Connie. She'd worried that her decision would push the woman she loved like a daughter out of her life, but in the end, she couldn't come up with any other way to guarantee all three of her sons returned to the Diamond Dust.

And then two days ago Aidan had offered Connie the job of events coordinator. Eventually, she would learn how to be the best events coordinator ever, Diane was certain of that, and it would ensure she'd always have a place at the winery. To everyone's shock, she'd not only declined the offer, but had quit her job at the Diamond Dust.

Fortunately, Matt had been able to convince her to stay. And to give him a chance to be in her and her two young daughters' lives.

Which was wonderful, especially considering that Diane suspected Matt had been the real reason Connie had quit in the first place.

But that didn't change the fact that their events coordinator knew more about grapes than caterers.

Diane stood and crossed to the sink to rinse out her cup before putting it in the dishwasher, her movements jerky. Aidan was angry. She understood that, accepted it. Just as she'd accept the consequences of her actions, of the mistakes she'd made. One of those being that if things didn't work out the way she wanted them to, he might never forgive her.

She shut the dishwasher door with more force than necessary. That was a chance she was willing to take, alienating her son. Alienating *another* son, since Matt still hadn't fully forgiven her for forcing him to be a part of the business.

"As much as you may not like it," she said, "Yvonne is the best person for this temporary job. I wouldn't have hired her if I didn't truly believe that."

"She showed me her contract, the agreement you

made with her on behalf of the Diamond Dust." He set his still full cup on the counter and crossed his arms. "I want you to break it."

Drying her hands on a tea towel, Diane slowly faced him. "I can't do that."

"Can't? Or won't?"

"Both. I've never gone back on my word and I certainly don't plan to start now. Besides, that contract isn't only between me and Yvonne, it's between the Diamond Dust and World Class Weddings, and the last thing we need is another breach of contract lawsuit."

"We wouldn't have to deal with any lawsuits if you hadn't forced Matt to break his contract with Queen's Valley. Nice that you never have to go back on your word, but you have no problem asking your sons to."

Okay, she deserved that. Queens' Valley being the vineyard in South Australia where Matt had been working until three weeks ago. And a lawsuit was a small price to pay for her getting what she wanted.

She laid a hand on his arm. It was a testament to his love and respect for her that he didn't pull away. "I realize this isn't an ideal situation, but it's only temporary. Surely you can put aside your own personal feelings and do what's best for the Diamond Dust?"

Under her fingers, the muscles in his arm tensed. "Don't I always?"

Yes. Yes, he did. And that was the problem. His rigid sense of responsibility and loyalty to his family and the winery had cost him his marriage. Now she would use those same traits to push him and Yvonne back together. The rest was up to them.

"Everything will work out," she promised, patting his arm. "You'll see."

He paced to the table, muttered under his breath, then whirled back to her. "You're playing matchmaker."

Since there was no use in denying it, she shrugged. "You and Yvonne were meant to be together."

"We were married," he snapped. "It ended. It wasn't some great tragic love story. It was a mistake. One I've been over for a long time now."

"If I believed that, I wouldn't have done this."

He nodded once, his mouth a thin, angry line. "When you pulled that stunt with Matt, threatening to sell the business unless he agreed to go into a partnership with us, I thought it was a shitty thing to do—"

"Yes, as I recall, you made your feelings about my decision quite clear."

"Even though I didn't agree with you, I stood by you. But there's no way I'm going to let you control my life. Not like you did to Matt. And just for the record, I don't like being manipulated."

"Of course not, dear," Diane said, somehow finding the courage to meet his gaze. "No one does."

He stormed out the French doors to the backyard. But unlike Matt, who would've slammed the door shut, Aidan barely made a sound when he left.

He'd always been that way, Diane thought as she wet a dishcloth and wrung the excess water from it, her hands shaking. Even as a child Aidan had been in control of his emotions. Couldn't he see she wasn't trying to hurt him?

Slapping the cloth down, she scrubbed the already shining counter. She'd seen how crushed he'd been when his marriage fell apart. He'd never gotten over that failure or the woman he'd loved.

Now he could correct his mistakes, give Yvonne a chance to correct hers, as well. And yes, maybe they'd even find love again thanks to what Aidan saw as Diane's meddling.

She'd brought Matt back, reminded him what it was like to be a part of his family after spending so many years on his own. To be accepted and wanted and welcomed by them. To be a part of his heritage.

It'd been easier with Brady. Her middle son had been so lost. Hurting too much, drinking to numb the pain. Wrapped up in his isolation. She'd given him the choice of either accepting help or moving off the Diamond Dust. Though she wasn't foolish or arrogant enough to believe her ultimatum had been the impetus Brady needed to turn his life around, she'd take her victories wherever she could get them.

Life was too short not to.

"HELLO, MS. DELISLE," a woman said in a voice heavily laced with the deep South, when Yvonne answered her cell phone that afternoon. "Your father would like to speak with you. Please hold." Must be her dad's new assistant.

There was a soft click, then classical music floated through the speaker—Mendelssohn's "Spring Song," if she wasn't mistaken. Yvonne tucked the phone between her shoulder and ear and picked up two of her suitcases. She carried them down a short hallway, past the tiny kitchen where she'd dumped her work binders, folders, inspiration boards and laptop on the table, to the bedroom at the back of the cottage.

Her temporary home sat deep in the woods, a good mile from the Sheppards' main house. It was small and sparsely furnished, but she didn't need much. As long as it had a bed, a closet, a shower and a TV with working cable, she'd be fine.

In the bedroom, she hefted the bags onto the double bed. She was staying whether Aidan liked it or not. Though she'd been tempted to give in to his demands, she hadn't. Hadn't given up her own wants to please him.

Not like she used to.

Her movements brisk, she flipped the lid of the larger case open. And he'd been so…shocked. As if the idea of her having the brains—or the backbone—to stand up for herself had never occurred to him.

Arrogant, stubborn man.

After another click on the phone, she heard her father's deep, commanding voice. "Yvonne. Hello."

"Hello, Daddy." She picked up a pile of neatly folded

underwear and carried it to the tall dresser next to the window. She could easily picture her father, the chairman of Delisle Enterprises, sitting behind his antique desk, the sun shining through the large window of his high-rise office. He'd be in one of his dark designer suits, the Windsor knot of his tie perfect, his light hair flecked with gray. "How are you?"

"I'd be better if I didn't have to listen to your mother complain that she hasn't heard from you in three days."

Of course. Yvonne should've known that Elaine Winston Delisle's next move would be to have her husband step in.

Yvonne put the underwear in the top drawer, then went back for more. "I'll be sure to call her today."

"See that you do. You know how she worries."

Yes, her mother certainly did that. But he did his fair share, as well. An only child, Yvonne bore the brunt of those worries, the bulk of their love and the weight of their expectations.

And though she loved them, could she really be blamed for escaping to Charleston after her divorce? Oh, she'd tried returning to Savannah, tried to go back to playing the part of dutiful daughter, had even become engaged to the man they'd handpicked for her. Until she'd realized that what she needed even more than her parents' approval was some freedom so she could finally just be herself.

"Now that I've delivered your mother's message," he continued, "how's my favorite girl?"

Not even the warmth and concerned note in her father's voice could shove Aidan's words from her head.

Daddy's little princess.

"I'm fine," she said, more sharply than necessary. She pressed her lips together. When she spoke again, her tone was carefully modulated. "Everything's fine, Daddy. Really."

And damn Aidan for making her feel as if she should be ashamed of her upbringing.

"I still think taking that job at that winery is a mistake," her father said.

"I appreciate your concern, I really do, but it's too late for objections." She dropped her bras onto the dresser. "I'm already here." And since she could practically hear his disapproval humming over the phone line, she added, "Besides, Joelle asked me to take on this assignment." Of course, Yvonne had been more than thrilled to accept when Joelle, the owner of World Class Weddings, had told her Diane had asked for her specifically. "And I signed a contract. You wouldn't want me to break it, would you?"

"When I taught you the importance of keeping your word, I didn't mean at the expense of your pride."

She smiled. "I still have my pride. This is just business." It wasn't as if she was crawling back to Aidan, begging him to give her a second chance. She was there on her terms.

"I hope you're right," Richard groused. "But promise

me you'll be careful. And that this business will remain just business."

"I promise." An easy enough pledge to make, considering the way Aidan had looked at her earlier. The only personal feelings that man had for her were contempt and anger. A lump formed in her throat and she cleared it away. "Try not to worry."

"Of course I worry. You're my little girl."

With a small eye roll, she set a white bra in the drawer, followed by a beige one. His "little girl" was a thirty-one-year-old divorcée with a thriving career and, she realized with a frown, an extensive collection of beige bras.

"I'm capable of taking care of myself," she said as kindly as she could.

"I know that. You're a Delisle, aren't you? I just don't want to see that bastard hurt you again."

She'd been the one to walk away from her marriage, but her father insisted on blaming Aidan for their divorce. Her mother, on the other hand, believed Yvonne had been a fool to leave a handsome, successful, intelligent man who'd done his best to take care of her.

Yvonne had learned early on it was futile to argue with either of them.

Besides, she couldn't honestly say either one was completely wrong.

"No one's going to get hurt." Least of all her. Not again. "I'm so sorry, Daddy, but I have a meeting to get to. I'll call Mother later today, okay? Bye, now. Love you."

She shut off her phone before he could respond.

Not exactly the mature, responsible or brave way of handling a difficult conversation, but an effective one nonetheless. For the time being, anyway.

And she wasn't lying, exactly, about her meeting. She just hadn't mentioned it wasn't for another half hour, that's all.

She lined up her bras in a neat row and shut the drawer. Someone knocked on the front door. Even as she stilled, her hand on the drawer handle, her pulse picked up. She wasn't expecting anyone. Then again, why would she be? Only one person knew she was here already.

She leaped for her purse on the bed, digging through it as she hurried into the bathroom. She touched up her lipstick, rubbed her lips together in lieu of blotting with a tissue, then ran her fingers through her hair before rushing down the hall and into the foyer.

More knocks—these rapid and impatient sounding.

"Coming," she called, slipping her right foot back into one of the black pumps she'd toed off after she'd brought the last of her luggage inside. With one hand on the wall for balance, she put on the left shoe. "Just a moment."

She straightened and swept back her hair. Inhaled a calming breath and opened the door.

Only to find it wasn't Aidan on the other side.

"Diane," she said, refusing to believe the unsettled feeling in her stomach was disappointment. "Hello."

Diane Sheppard held a recyclable grocery bag in each hand, her smile small and polite. Detached. The same smile Yvonne often used when faced with an acquaintance she didn't know very well. One she didn't particularly care to know better.

"I thought I'd drop by," Diane was saying. "Save you the trouble of coming over to the house and…" She lifted the bags. "I wasn't sure when you'd have a chance to get into town so I picked up some groceries."

Yvonne's mouth popped open. "Oh. That was very…"

The other woman stepped forward, leaving her no choice but to move out her way.

"Thoughtful," she finished lamely as Diane entered the house and headed straight for the kitchen.

Yvonne glanced from Diane's retreating back to the porch and back again.

What just happened?

"Are you getting settled in all right?" Diane called from the other room.

The other room where Yvonne had piled boxes and papers and folders and files on the kitchen table to get them out of the way. Horrified, she quickly shut the door and a moment later found Diane unloading groceries onto the counter.

"Uh…yeah." Yvonne winced and cleared her throat

as she tried to straighten up the mess on the table. "I mean, yes. Thank you so much for asking."

Heat crawled up her neck. So much for her hope that after seven years she'd be more at ease around her daunting mother-in-law.

Ex. *Ex*-mother-in-law.

They had no ties. Not anymore. Had really had none even when they'd been related. Diane had always been pleasant to her, but their relationship had been merely… cordial. Their only common ground had been their mutual love for Aidan. Now, facing Diane, Yvonne had no idea what to do next. Offer her hand? Too formal. A hug? Oh, God, that was inconceivable.

"Good." Diane handed her a small bunch of green bananas. "If you need anything, don't hesitate to call," she said, somehow making what from anyone else would be a request sound like an order.

Yvonne stared down at the fruit. What was she supposed to do with it? She didn't even like bananas. "I will," she answered calmly, when what she really wanted to do was shove Diane out the door so she could compose herself. Tidy up the cottage. Realign her thoughts to accommodate the fact that her schedule, her plan for the afternoon, had been changed. "And thank you for the groceries. I hope you didn't go to too much trouble, though."

"No trouble at all." Diane set a box of shredded wheat cereal in an upper cabinet. "I was at the store and tossed a few essentials in for you. And since I baked yesterday,

I brought some cookies as well." She glanced over her shoulder. "Chocolate chip."

Aidan's favorite.

"How...nice," Yvonne managed to say lightly. "I'm sure I'll enjoy them."

And maybe as she ate them, she could remember how she'd gotten Diane's recipe and made a batch herself. Because Aidan had asked her to. Her first—and last—attempt at baking had ended with smoke billowing from the oven, a visit from the local fire department and her feeling like a complete failure.

"Aidan mentioned you were at the carriage house this morning," Diane said, opening the refrigerator door and putting away the milk and butter.

"I got in early and thought I'd check out the building." She scraped off the sticker on the bananas and rolled it into a tube. "He seemed quite surprised to hear I'd been hired."

"Hmm...yes...well, that's probably because I hadn't told him yet."

Yvonne set the bananas on the only bare corner of the table. "He doesn't want me here."

"No. He certainly doesn't." Diane stacked one bag on top of the other and then folded them. "But I do."

Ducking her head, Yvonne examined the bananas closer. "I appreciate your belief in my abilities. I'll do everything in my power to make sure your wedding is perfect."

"Oh, I have no doubt. Which is why I'm confident everything will turn out as I'd planned."

Why Diane's expression was just this side of sly, Yvonne had no idea. Wasn't sure she wanted to know. It was enough that Diane had asked her here. She finally had the chance to make a real connection with a woman she'd always respected, but who'd never accepted her.

"That's why I'm here," she said with her most professional smile. "To make sure you get everything you want for your business and your wedding."

"What I want is for my wedding to be the first official event held at the Diamond Dust—a sort of kickoff to our venture into hosting. Al and I have both been married before, so we don't need all the pomp and circumstance this time around. We want a small, intimate gathering with our families and closest friends. And we want it to showcase the best of the winery so people can see what to expect if they hold their own special events here."

Right. Could she pull this off?

Yvonne's smile felt stiff and cold. Or maybe the panic squeezing her throat was cutting off the blood supply to her face. "No problem."

Diane nodded. "I know this is short notice, so I'm sure you're anxious to get started. Why don't you stop by the house tomorrow for lunch? I'll have a finalized guest list for you by then."

"That'll be fine," she said, calculating in her head how much time she had to get the invitations ordered and sent. Not enough. Not nearly enough. She moved aside the scrapbook she'd made showcasing some of her most successful weddings, so she could pick up the large binder underneath. "I have some invitation samples here," she said, laying the open binder on the counter. "Once you find a design you like, we can customize the colors and—"

"Whatever you pick will be fine."

In the act of flipping to a design she thought Diane would like, Yvonne froze. "Excuse me?"

"Naturally Al and I will let you know the wording we'd like to use, but the design, the colors…" the older woman waved her hand. "Those are up to you."

"You want me to choose your wedding invitations?" she asked incredulously.

This time Diane's smile was warm, her eyes lit with humor. "Isn't that what wedding planners do?"

"I help people make choices about flowers and color schemes and menus and music," Yvonne said slowly. "Everything that enables them to have their dream wedding. Those choices are based on the client's preferences and their budget."

Diane crossed her arms over her ample chest and studied Yvonne over her glasses. "My preference is that you plan my wedding—all aspects of it, except for my dress, which I've already picked out."

"But…but what about your attendants' dresses? Tuxes for the men? Favors and—"

"Al and I are having our children stand up for us. It

would probably be best if you let Marsha, Al's daughter, pick her own dress based on the color scheme you choose, but the boys can wear suits. As for favors…" Diane grimaced, as if a token gift of appreciation was on par with finding someone else's hair in your dinner. "I've never been big on that sort of thing. Let's just skip that part?"

Yvonne realized she was staring at her with her mouth open. She snapped her lips together. This was crazy. She'd had carefree, laid-back brides before, but nothing like this.

"I'm not sure I feel comfortable taking over that way." She was excellent at making a client's dreams come true.

How could she do that for Diane if they didn't work together?

"Why don't you put together your ideas and I'll approve them."

"I don't—"

"I'd really like your help with all this."

And that was the whole reason she was here. Diane needed her. "All right," Yvonne said. The decision seemed somehow life-altering. Then again, maybe all stupid decisions seemed that way at first. "I'll have a few sample invitations ready for you to look at during lunch tomorrow. Maybe we can also discuss some ideas I have for advertising events at the winery."

She'd spent the entire five and a half hour drive from Charleston brainstorming ways to promote the new venture. She wanted to be prepared, to do a good job. Plus it'd kept her from thinking about what a possibly colossal mistake coming back here was.

"I'm not really involved in all that," Diane said as she headed toward the door.

Frowning, Yvonne followed her. "You're not?"

"No. You'll have to discuss any changes or ideas with Aidan."

Yvonne curled her fingers into her palms. "But you hired me." She'd thought she'd be working with Diane. Yes, she'd realized she'd have to be around Aidan, but for the chance to finally be accepted at the Diamond Dust by Diane, she'd been willing to risk it.

"Your contract is with the winery, which Aidan runs. For the next few months, anyway." Yvonne must've looked as horrified as she felt, because Diane's expression softened. "Don't worry. He'll treat you fairly."

"How can you be sure?"

She shrugged, then opened the door. "Because you're what's best for the company. Aidan always does what's best for the Diamond Dust."

CHAPTER THREE

THOUGH THE DOOR to Aidan's office was open in welcome, Yvonne couldn't force her feet forward. One
thing was for certain, that welcome wasn't meant for
her.

She squeezed her eyes shut, hard. When she opened
them again, spots danced in her vision. Those spots, she
reminded herself, were like her memories. Real enough,
yes. But quick to fade.

Elongating her spine as she'd been taught during her
years on the pageant circuit, she raised her hand to tap
on the door frame, then caught sight of Aidan staring
out the window.

She slowly lowered her arm. The sunlight picked
up the golden threads in his hair, and though his hands
were in his pockets, one hip leaning against the windowsill, there was still an…edge to him. A hardness he
couldn't hide even when he thought he was all alone.
The same hardness she'd detected in him earlier.

She was afraid she was the cause of it.

As if sensing her presence, he stiffened and turned,
catching her staring at him like a lovesick newlywed.
It was as if she was transported back to when her entire

world had revolved around him. When all she'd cared about was making him happy, and her greatest fear had been of not being the woman he wanted her to be.

She bit the inside of her cheek.

"Do you have a minute?" she asked, when it was obvious he wasn't going to invite her in.

He wanted to say no. She could see that clearly in the set of his jaw. The coolness in his eyes. Instead, he inclined his head. An affirmation? In condescension? She wasn't sure.

She stepped into the room. He didn't move, but looked her over from the top of her freshly heat-ironed hair to the ruffle on her blouse and the edge of her skirt at her knees. Her scalp prickled.

And when something cold and wet nudged her hand, she about jumped right out of her Jimmy Choos and hit the ceiling.

Her heart in her throat, she glanced down at a large dog with brown eyes and shiny, rust-colored fur. She lifted her hand to her mouth, biting gently on the knuckle of her forefinger—something she hadn't done since she was ten and had finally given in to her mother's constant nagging and broken the bad habit. She dropped her hand. The dog barked and Yvonne recoiled.

"She won't hurt you."

Unwilling to take her eyes off the dog—or those teeth—for more than a second, Yvonne didn't so much as glance at Aidan. "No. I...I'm sure she won't."

Except that for every hesitant step back Yvonne took, the dog took one forward.

"Lily," Aidan said in his deep voice. "Come here."

The dog—Lily—sniffed at the laptop Yvonne gripped in her hand. Sweat broke out along her hairline. She hoped Aidan couldn't hear the wild thumping of her heart.

Aidan, however, with his watchful eyes and quick mind, never missed anything.

He snapped his fingers. "Lily. Now."

After one more sniff, the dog padded over to him. He patted her head—as a reward for obeying him or because the dog hadn't ripped Yvonne's hand off at the wrist, she didn't know.

Maybe both.

"I…" She swallowed and tried again. "I didn't know you had a…a dog."

Unrolling the sleeves of his denim shirt, he raised his eyebrows. "I hadn't realized I was to keep you abreast of any pets I may or may not have. Or did I miss something in our divorce agreement?"

She blushed furiously. "No. No, of course not. I just… I had no idea you liked—" she glanced at the dog, which seemed to be watching her with more interest than was warranted "—animals."

"Now you do."

"Right." But…what else didn't she know about him? After all, it'd been almost seven years since she'd seen him last. A lot could happen in that amount of time. A

lump formed in her throat. Oh, dear Lord. "Did you...
have you remarried?" she asked, looking around the
room for signs of a wife.

She cringed. But it was too late to take her question
back, much as she would like to.

He paused in the act of buttoning his sleeve. "No."

She felt light-headed. "Oh. That's..." What? A relief?
A disappointment? She wasn't sure which one would be
the bigger lie. "I was engaged," she heard herself blurt
out, the nails of her free hand digging into her palm.
"It didn't work out."

Aidan went completely still. For a moment she wondered if he was even breathing. But then he lifted his
head and his expression was so dispassionate, goose
bumps rose on her arms. "I don't remember asking."

No. Of course he hadn't. Why did she bring it up?
She hardly enjoyed discussing her broken engagement
or her ex-fiancé—the man her parents had chosen for
her once her divorce from Aidan had been final. A man
who'd wanted her because of her name.

She needed to stay calm and get her rioting emotions
under control before he saw through her facade and took
that control away from her.

Yvonne smiled, professional, confident and totally
fake. "I was hoping we could go over a few things—if
you have time, that is."

"Actually, I'm in the middle of something."

Her expression never faltered. "Yes, I could see how

busy you were when I came in. But, perhaps when you do get a free minute, we could—"

"My schedule seems to be full for the next few days," he said, crossing his arms. "Sorry."

She set her free hand on her hip. "Diane said you were running the winery. That I had to speak to you about any ideas regarding hosting events."

"That's right."

"So when, exactly," she said through barely moving lips, "can this conversation take place?"

He crossed to his massive mahogany desk and flipped a page of his appointment book. "I can give you thirty minutes Monday morning at eight."

"But that's—" she did a quick calculation. "—five days from now."

"Look at that. All those accounting classes did pay off."

"I have only six weeks to get your mother's wedding planned," she said in carefully modulated tones. "I can't wait until Monday."

"It's the best I can do."

Had she forgotten how stubborn he was? "In that case," she said, all sweetness and light while she clutched her laptop case, "Monday will be fine."

"Have a list of the topics you want to discuss, along with your ideas, to me by Friday."

"So you won't have to spend any more time in my company than necessary?"

He sat on the thronelike leather chair and leaned

back. The flat line of his mouth and the way he studied her gave her the answer to her question. "I guess I'll see you Monday then."

She blushed. He was dismissing her. Oh, it was polite enough, she supposed, but it still felt as if he'd put a foot to her rear and given her a good shove.

Yvonne turned and even took a step toward the door before facing him again. "Maybe it would help if we got a few things out in the open."

"Help what?"

"Help ease this…awkwardness."

Awkwardness she couldn't stand. That made her want to hide within herself so she wouldn't do or say anything to make things worse.

Except he didn't seem to be uncomfortable in the least. His hands were linked together on his flat stomach, his shoulders relaxed. The only sign he wasn't less than perfectly put together were the slight wrinkles on his sleeves from having rolled them up earlier.

Some things never changed. As always, he was calm, his thoughts neatly hidden, his feelings under wraps. While she fought not to show how frazzled she was, how worried that she'd say the wrong thing.

"Your mother assured me I'll be treated fairly and without bias while I'm here," Yvonne said, sounding even to her own ears like the petulant princess Aidan thought she was.

"But you doubt her word?"

"Not at all." She'd be a fool to doubt what Diane said.

Besides, she wanted to believe her job here could go smoothly. "But I'd like to hear it from you."

He sat up slowly. "Hear what, exactly?"

"That you'll be fair. That you're going to give me a chance to do my job."

She had to force herself not to squirm under his watchful gaze. "I can guarantee that you'll be treated like any other employee."

"But I'm not any other employee. I was your wife."

His eyes narrowed to slits. "*Was* being the operative word."

Her heart pounded so hard, she was sure he could see it fluttering the ruffles on her shirt. "*Wife* being the important one. I want to make sure we can work together."

"You really don't know why my mother hired you, do you?"

Though suddenly uneasy, she kept any hint of it out of her tone. "She hired me to plan her wedding. And because the Diamond Dust needs someone to help coordinate events."

"We only decided to start hosting events Sunday night—and before you start counting, that was three days ago. And, out of all the events coordinators in the South, she hired you. It never occurred to you to wonder why?"

Yvonne brushed a dog hair from her skirt. "She needed someone with experience who was willing to relocate—"

"She hired you," he said flatly, "because she thinks if we work together, you'll get back in my life. She hired you because she wants us to get together again."

PANIC FLARED IN Yvonne's dark eyes. But she remained steady on those pencil-thin high heels of hers. "I'm sorry," she said, as if they were discussing whether to have salmon or chicken for dinner, "I don't understand."

His curled fists hidden from view under his desk, Aidan studied her. As if she didn't have a care in the world, was above everything he said.

If that was true, why did her fingers tremble when she swept her hair off her shoulder?

He wasn't the only one out of sorts. Good.

"Seeing as how you're not stupid or hard of hearing," he said mildly, "you understand perfectly."

Her mouth turned down. "Diane wants us back together?"

Aidan held her gaze as he straightened in his chair. "Or maybe you already knew that."

"Excuse me?" she asked, sounding as snobby and cold as her mother had when Aidan and Yvonne went to Savannah and announced their engagement to her parents.

But he'd been so sure Yvonne was different from her mom. That underneath that cool demeanor was a real, live woman. And all he had to do was help warm her up.

"Have you missed me, Yvonne? Are you looking for a reconciliation?"

She didn't blush or appear guilty. She just looked… scared. As if the idea of getting back together with him was worse than having her fingernails ripped off. His mouth twisted. Right. Because living with him had been such pure hell. It'd been so bad she'd walked off without so much as giving him a chance to convince her to stay.

"I assure you," she said, no longer sounding in control, "I had no idea. I…" She pressed her lips together. "I thought Diane hired me because I'm a good wedding planner."

She seemed sincere. Hell, he probably would have believed her if he hadn't already learned not to trust anything she said.

I love you. Till death do us part, she'd vowed at their wedding.

She could claim the earth was round and he'd want a second opinion.

He picked up his mechanical pencil and tapped it against the top of his desk, causing Lily to raise her head. "Now that you're aware of Mom's real agenda, I'm sure you'll agree that backing out of your contract is the only option."

Yvonne frowned and shifted, the movement causing her breasts to sway slightly under the ruffle of her top, drawing his attention to the way that damn skirt hugged her hips. In stark black and white, the severe lines of the skirt contrasting with the soft femininity of her top, highlighted her sexy elegance. As if nothing and no one could touch her.

Good thing he didn't want to try.

"I can't do that," she said quietly. "I'm sorry. I truly am, and I realize this situation is…uncomfortable…for both of us, but I'm staying."

"Did you get fired?"

Her lips twitched. "No, I'm gainfully employed."

"Then there's no reason you can't return to Charleston."

"None at all. And I will when I've met my obligation here. Until then, can't we figure out a way to make this work?" She began to lift her laptop case. "If we could get past—"

She broke off when Lily, excited that the new person in the room was moving, got up and walked over to sniff at Yvonne's backside. Yvonne froze, her face white.

Damn it. He didn't want to see her afraid. Didn't like the tug of sympathy that caused in him. How it made him feel…protective of her.

"Lily, sit," he ordered, more gruffly than necessary.

Lily lowered her head and crept back to her spot by the window. He rubbed the nape of his neck. Great. Now he was taking his irritation out on his dog.

"Since you insist on sticking around," he said tightly, "you'll have to get used to Lily. She has free run of the Diamond Dust. And I'm not about to keep her locked up because you don't like animals."

"No. Of course not. I would never ask you to keep

it…her…" Yvonne paused long enough to take a deep breath and regain her composure. "I'm sorry. I…I don't have much experience with animals…with pets. Mother never allowed them."

No doubt Elaine Delisle thought pets were too messy. "Luckily, my family doesn't share your mother's opinion. There have always been dogs at the vineyard."

"There weren't any…"

Before. When they'd first moved to Jewell after his father became sick. When they were still married. Before she'd walked out on their marriage.

"Mom hadn't wanted to get another dog after their last one died." He tossed his pencil aside and got to his feet, unable to remain seated. "Too painful."

Yvonne nodded as if she completely understood, playing the part of concerned, sympathetic ex for all she was worth. She was excellent at all her roles, whatever they may be. Obedient daughter. Beauty queen.

Aidan had thought he'd known her better than anyone else ever would. Ever could. Until she'd left and he'd realized he hadn't known her at all.

She cleared her throat, glancing at Lily with clear trepidation. "As you can see, I'm a bit…nervous around dogs."

Not his problem. It wasn't up to him to make her feel safe. Happy.

But as much as he didn't want her here, he couldn't let her think that every time she stepped outside her door, she was risking being torn apart by his good-natured dog. He wasn't that big of an ass. No matter what his brothers said about him.

He snapped his fingers and Lily padded over and sat next to his leg. "Lily's a good dog. Sweet as they come and well-trained—"

"I didn't mean to imply—"

"I know," he said, "that you didn't mean to imply I didn't train my dog. I'm saying that she won't hurt you. You have my word on that."

Yvonne smiled, relieved. She trusted him.

It nearly undid him.

He scowled and her smile faded. She switched the laptop case to her other hand. "I appreciate that. Especially as I know you're a man who always keeps his word."

"Funny thing about that…once I make a promise, I keep it." He searched her face, her beautiful, treacherous face.

Her flinch was slight, but noticeable, letting him know his dig had hit home. He didn't find much satisfaction in it.

Then she tipped her head. "Not everyone has your conviction, or your sense of responsibility and right and wrong," she said, so sweetly, he didn't believe she meant a word of it. "And sometimes, keeping a promise means giving up something a person isn't willing to lose."

He narrowed his eyes. What the hell was that supposed to mean? Was she talking about their marriage, as he had been, and her choice to break her vows? He concentrated on keeping his breathing slow and even, pretended his chest wasn't tight, his muscles not tensed.

He'd never asked her to give up anything for him—except living in Savannah. But she'd been all for moving to Jewell to help his parents during his father's illness. She'd even suggested they buy a house, to make the move more permanent. She'd wanted their own place, she'd told him. Their own home. A place where they belonged.

"Guess that's what they call making a sacrifice," he said. And he didn't plan on sacrificing his peace of mind for the next two months, or fall blindly in line with his mother's plans. "You came in here to get some sort of guarantee I'd treat you fairly. Let me just say that during your stint here, I'll treat you cordially and with the respect you deserve." There was nothing in his tone that suggested that amount of respect would be little to none. "And that's a promise."

One he could make without any worries about risking his pride. Or his heart. He never made the same mistake twice.

He sat back down and put on his reading glasses with one hand, while picking up a random piece of paper with the other. "Now, if you'll excuse me, I have a lot of work to do before I can go home, and I'd like to get back to it."

He pretended to study the paper—an invoice Matt had given him earlier for the cost of new plantings. She didn't call him on how she'd walked in on him doing nothing more than staring out the window, but she also didn't leave. He turned to his computer and moved the mouse to wake it from sleep mode.

After a few moments, she finally turned and walked away.

Thank God.

YVONNE DESCENDED THE last step into the foyer, her jaw so tight it ached.

Bastard.

But she couldn't let him see how furious he made her. Or worse, how much his obvious dislike for her hurt.

Here she was, back in a place where she'd never felt she truly belonged, surrounded by people she'd suspected never really wanted her here.

Not much had changed, it seemed.

She'd been... God, she'd been so...so arrogant. Had seriously thought that Diane needed her. Had imagined how she'd sweep in with her schedules and grand plans and experience and organize their efforts. That Diane's wedding would be the talk of the South, and the Diamond Dust would be set up as the premier place to hold events in Southern Virginia. Maybe in the entire state.

All thanks to Yvonne.

Showing them all she was more than just the spoiled rich girl Aidan had brought home. The one who'd never fit in.

But Diane didn't need her. She was using her because of her past with Aidan.

At least that was a new one. Usually people wanted her in their lives because of her name, her wealth, her connections or her looks.

No one ever wanted her for herself.

She was halfway to the front door when someone rounded the corner behind her at the back of the house.

"What the hell are you doing here?"

As with Aidan earlier that day, this voice was familiar to her. Except it belonged to a woman. One she would've been happy to have gone her entire stay in Jewell without ever laying eyes on.

No such luck.

Pasting on a fake, toothy smile, the one she'd used to perfection during her pageant days, she faced Connie Henkel. "That's the second time I've been greeted with those same words," she said, intensifying her accent. She knew the drawl would irritate the other woman no end. "Does everyone here have something against a simple hello? Or maybe y'all just lack manners?"

She immediately regretted her snide comment when Connie's eyes narrowed, giving her the look of a sleek cat. A dangerous one. And, Yvonne had to admit with an inner sigh, a sexy, confident one in her tight jeans and snug T-shirt the color of a ripe plum. The collar of her own formal blouse suddenly choked her.

Connie had always made her feel as snobbish and uptight as her mother. Like Diane, the other woman intimidated her, pure and simple. She'd fit here, with the Sheppards.

A tall, broad-shouldered man came up behind Connie and the woman whirled around to demand, "What the hell is she doing here?"

He looked over her head at Yvonne, his eyes widening. "Don't blame me. I had nothing to do with it. But if she sticks around, it'd knock Aidan on his ass." He smiled at Yvonne. "Please tell me you plan on sticking around."

It was that grin that helped her realize why he looked so familiar. "Matt?" she asked, taking in the changes seven years had made in the youngest Sheppard's appearance. Gone was the gangly, baby-faced charmer. Now Matt's face was leaner, his cheeks and chin covered in dark blond stubble, his long, wheat-colored hair held back in a ponytail.

"One and only," he assured her with a wink.

Connie sent him a scathing glare. "Really? You're flirting now? With *her?*"

He slung a companionable arm around Connie's shoulders. "Now, sugar, you know you're the only woman I flirt with," he said, and though his tone was teasing, the heat in his eyes when he looked at Connie said there was more going on between these two than friendship. A lot sure had changed around here. "I'm being friendly. After all, Yvonne used to be family."

"Used to be," Connie muttered, crossing her arms as yet another man came around the corner from what Yvonne remembered was a large family room-kitchen area.

He was a few inches shorter than Matt, his hair lighter and cropped close to his head, his eyes blue to his younger brother's green. But the shape of his nose, the sharp angle of his jaw and the confidence in his posture gave him away as a Sheppard.

"Hello, Brady," she said. "So nice to see you."

He blinked—the only sign he gave of being surprised to find her in his mother's foyer. "Yvonne."

"Please tell me you just happened to be passing through town." Connie stepped toward Yvonne, brushing off Matt's arm. "And that you're now on your way back to…wherever it is you took off to before."

She looked so hopeful—almost as hopeful as Yvonne had felt about her six weeks here. Before she'd found out Diane was only using her.

"Oh, Connie, I'm sorry to have to disappoint you…" She was even sorrier to face that same disappointment herself. "But I've accepted a position here for the next two months. And may I just say," she added, keeping all trace of sarcasm out of her voice, "how much I'm… looking forward to working with you all."

She ended her performance with a soft smile, her expression composed, her grip on her laptop relaxed.

Brady and Matt exchanged a quick, loaded look, while Connie's mouth worked but no words came out.

Then she took off up the stairs, her long legs taking the steps two at a time. "Aidan!"

"Well," Yvonne said brightly to the two men staring at her, "I should get going as well. It was lovely to see you both."

CHAPTER FOUR

TWENTY MINUTES LATER, Connie paced between Aidan's desk and the matching leather chairs where Brady and Matt sat. He'd asked them all to his office at the end of the workday so he could explain about Diane hiring Yvonne and moving up her wedding date. He'd been as quick and concise as possible, leaving out only a few minor details. Such as how seeing Yvonne again had tied him in knots.

"I don't trust her," Connie said, her strides not slowing in the least. "She'll stab us in the back. You wait and see."

Aidan rubbed at the headache brewing behind his temples, and leaned back in his chair. "How would she do that? Sabotage Mom and Al's wedding?"

"I don't know." Connie tossed her hands in the air, her slim body vibrating with rage. "She could...order the wrong flowers. Or...or mess up the cake on purpose."

"I hate to say it," Matt interjected lazily, "but you're sounding a bit paranoid."

"He's right." Aidan held up a conciliatory hand when she looked ready to leap down Matt's throat and rip his heart out. "Yvonne's not going to do anything to ruin the wedding or risk it not being perfect. After all, she has as much to gain from it being a success as the Diamond Dust does. And she'd never do anything to hurt her own reputation."

Not when appearances were everything to her.

"I'm not paranoid." Connie sniffed. "That...woman isn't good for the winery."

"I think we're all in agreement on that," Aidan said. "But it's only for two months. The best way to handle it is to treat her as if she's any other employee. If we all remain focused and do our jobs, having her here won't be a big deal."

Connie gave him a look that clearly said she thought he'd been dropped on his head as a baby. "That's easy for you to say. You don't have to work with her."

He picked up a pen and held it tightly with both hands. Easy for him? Not even close.

"Seeing as how there's nothing we can do about it," he said, "I don't see any reason to let it...to let her... bother us. All we have to do is get through the next two months, then she'll be gone and it'll be as if she was never here in the first place."

Like before.

"What was your mother thinking?" Connie muttered, obviously not willing to take his damned good advice. "How could she do this?"

"You'll have to ask her." It was the same thing he'd

said to Matt when he'd asked why their mother was blackmailing him to take part in the business.

No way was Aidan explaining that she was now playing Cupid. Hell, knowing that would push Connie right over the edge.

Matt raised his hand and pointed at his watch. "You want me to pick up the girls?" he asked, referring to Connie's two young daughters.

"No. I'll go. I need to stop by the bank anyway." She jabbed a finger at Aidan. "This conversation isn't over."

"How about instead of you actually finishing it with me," Aidan said somberly, "you say your piece to Matt, then he can give me the condensed version. I just don't see why I should be punished," he continued, when Connie growled at him. "Since none of this is my fault."

"You married that…her," she said. "So don't try and say this isn't somehow your fault."

And with that, the closest friend he had, the woman who'd stuck by his side during his father's illness and death, and the crumbling of his marriage, turned and left.

"If you don't relax," Matt said in his slow, irritating drawl, "you're going to break that pen. And we all know how you'd hate to get even a speck of ink one of your pristine shirts."

Aidan glanced down to see his hands were shaking. He carefully set the pen down. "You're loving this, aren't you?"

Matt rubbed his fingertips over his cheek thoughtfully, as if just noticing he needed a shave. Aidan wished he'd notice he needed a haircut, too.

"Well, now," his brother said, "*love* is a strong word. Although I am enjoying the hell out of seeing you squirm."

"That's because you're an ass," Aidan said flatly. Brady inclined his head in agreement.

"I'm just glad I'm not the only one whose life Mom is trying to control." Matt stood and stretched his arms overhead until his back cracked. "Look, it sucks. I know that better than anyone. But at least it's a temporary situation. One I'm sure you'll get through without so much as a hair out of place."

"Right. Unlike you, who was forced to stay. Tell me, does Connie know what a struggle it must be for you to get through each day, how you're obviously resigned to your fate? Because I was under the impression you were actually happy with the way things turned out."

"I am." Shrugging, he grinned. "But just because a man likes his final destination doesn't mean the trip getting there was painless. I'm sure the survivors of the *Titanic* would agree."

"Profound."

"You want my advice?"

"The day I do is the day they'd better put me in the ground."

"Don't fight it—it's like one of those choke collars. The harder you struggle, the tighter the damn thing gets. Keep your head down and get through each day one minute at a time."

Then, with a sharp salute, his cocky brother backed out of the room.

"He has a point," Brady said.

"You don't say one word up until now and that's how you break your silence?"

"He's right about keeping your head down. If you don't play Mom's game, you can't lose. Unless you *want* to reconcile with Yvonne?"

Studying his brother's stoic expression, Aidan slid to the edge of his seat. "You know."

Brady straightened his left leg. "There's no other reason for Mom to bring your ex-wife here except to try and get you two back together."

"Guess she's feeling cocky after her recent victory over Matt."

"I lucked out. Mom only threatened to kick me off the Diamond Dust," Brady murmured. "You want me to talk to her?"

Aidan snapped his head up so quickly he about broke his neck. "You're offering to have a conversation with someone? The man of as few words as possible."

"Doesn't mean I don't get my point across."

True. "I appreciate the sentiment, but don't bother. It wouldn't work, anyway. I've already spoken with Mom and she's set on this. And we both know once she's made up her mind, there's no changing it."

It was a stubbornness they all shared. Which didn't make it less annoying, just easier to recognize.

"Besides," Aidan continued, "it's not like I have to go along with Mom's little scheme." He didn't have to fall for Yvonne. Not again. "Yvonne and I ended it a long time ago. Believe me, neither one of is us interested in revisiting our relationship."

Brady tapped his fingers against his thigh. Opened his mouth, then shut it again.

Aidan raised his eyebrows. "You going to spit out whatever it is you're chewing on? Or would you rather I guess?"

His brother shifted. "Be careful."

"Of Yvonne?"

"Of your feelings for her."

"I don't have any feelings for her." Aidan stood, his chair slamming into the bookcases behind him with a sharp crack.

There was one second of blessed silence as Brady smiled. "Yeah. I can see that."

Tucking his fisted hands behind his back, Aidan drew in a deep breath. "We were married," he pointed out in what he thought was a rational, dispassionate tone—one that hid the turmoil bubbling inside him, "but that doesn't mean I'm holding on to some sort of… infatuation…after all these years."

"Keep it that way. Don't hold on to something that died long ago."

"This isn't like you and Liz."

Liz Montgomery had been Brady's fiancée—until a year ago, when she'd written him a Dear John letter while he'd been serving with the marines in Afghanistan. Shortly after, he'd been injured during a routine patrol and his life had spiraled violently out of control, resulting in a drunken Brady crashing Liz's wedding this past summer. He'd ended up in bed with Liz's younger sister, Jane Cleo—a one-night stand that ended in pregnancy. Brady and J.C. were married a few weeks ago.

"I appreciate your concern," Aidan added, "but I'm fine. It's not as if I've spent the past seven years obsessed with getting Yvonne back. I moved on."

"Good," Brady said, as he walked toward the door.

"Besides," Aidan called, "it's for just a little over a month. When it's over, she'll leave."

Again.

Though Brady didn't turn around, his voice carried quite clearly back to Aidan even as he stepped out into the hall. "You sure about that?"

Damn right he was sure. Aidan began to pace, and Lily, lying in a patch of sun in front of the window, got to her feet, her tail wagging as she joined him. Yvonne wouldn't stay. He wouldn't allow it. And when it was all said and done, that was what mattered most. What he would and wouldn't allow.

Ownership of the Diamond Dust was to be transferred to him and his brothers at the end of July, but now that his mother had moved her wedding date up, he'd just have to make sure the partnership agreement was moved up, as well. Then it wouldn't matter what sort of agreement Yvonne made with his mom. He'd have control—diluted only by his brothers' two-thirds ownership.

But he wasn't going to take any chances. Not on something this important. He'd do everything he could to make sure Yvonne had no reason to stay in Jewell.

SHE WASN'T VAIN, Diane thought firmly later that night as she stared at herself in the full-length mirror in her bedroom, by the light coming through the open bathroom door. She'd always been too pragmatic, too honest to indulge in vanity. The way she looked, how she presented herself, had always taken a backseat to more important things. Her family. Her business. Who she was inside.

Her teeth chattered. Goose bumps rose on her damp legs and arms, prickled her skin like tiny pins. Water dripped from her slicked-back hair onto her bare shoulders. A drop trailed over her collarbone and down her chest, where it was absorbed by the towel she held clutched at her breasts.

But though she trembled with the cold, she didn't move. After years of giving her reflection no more than a passing glance, she couldn't look away from the woman before her. Her blond hair with its straggly, unmanageable grays. Her rounded shoulders.

What had happened to her?

She'd always enjoyed being a woman. Having strength and softness. Being loved by a man, desired by him. But that didn't mean she'd ever, even once, told herself that she needed those things in order to be whole. To have a fulfilling life.

Behind her, her fiancé slept in her large, warm bed. But no matter how much she wanted to, she couldn't lie with him there when she didn't even know herself anymore.

They hadn't made love in over three weeks. Every time Al reached for her, she claimed she was too tired. Too stressed first about Brady's wedding a few weeks back, then about planning their own wedding. Her thoughts were too consumed with her impending retirement and her sons taking over the winery. Al was always understanding. Patient. His love for her never wavered.

But instead of being grateful to have found love a second time with a wonderful man, all she felt was guilty. Because she was lying to him and everyone else. Yes, she was tired and stressed and worried…so very worried. But mostly, she didn't want to be touched. Didn't think she could bear it.

With a deep a breath, she forced her fingers to straighten, and the towel dropped to the thick carpet.

No, she'd never been a beauty, but she'd always had her own appeal. Clear skin. Wavy hair. And curves that had garnered more than her share of interest.

She slowly turned to the side and studied her profile. Those curves had expanded by about, oh, twenty pounds or so. She could blame her protruding stomach on the slowing of her metabolism, but knew it had more to do with her love of baking. And her even greater love of eating the treats she made. Her legs were still toned, thanks to her daily three-mile walks, but her waist was thicker, her hips rounder.

Not a perfect body but one that she'd taken good care of over the years. She'd given birth to three babies and nourished them during their first year of life. Her legs had supported her; her back was strong. She'd comforted her children, hugged them with joy and pride, and held her husband when he took his last breath. No, her body was far from perfect, but it'd always been limber and healthy.

The bedcovers rustled, and a moment later, Al flipped on the bedside lamp. She watched herself wince as the light brought her reflection into sharp relief.

"Honey?" he asked, his voice husky from his having drifted off while she'd been showering. "Are you all right?"

Her throat closed, making it impossible for her to swallow, let alone speak.

She sensed him moving, heard the sounds of him flipping the covers back and getting out of bed. A moment later, his reflection joined hers as he stood behind her, his short silver hair sticking up on the side, his white T-shirt wrinkled, his expression concerned. And loving. So much love.

"Diane?" He gently laid his hands on her bare shoulders, hurt crossing his face when she eased forward, away from his touch.

"What happened to me?" she murmured.

"I'm afraid I don't understand."

That was Al. If he didn't understand, he said so. He was happy to stand back and gather all the information he needed before offering his advice or a helping hand. Not so with Tom. He'd preferred action over words. If she had a problem, he would do everything in his power to fix it for her. Never mind that half the time he'd had no idea what he was fixing. He'd loved her. And while she couldn't honestly say he would've liked Al had they known each other, he would want her to move on with her life. To be happy and loved again.

Even for a short time.

"How did I turn into that?" she asked with a nod toward her reflection. "One day I woke up and there was this strange woman staring back at me from the mirror. I don't even recognize myself."

Al didn't try to touch her again, but he did step closer so that she could feel his body heat at her back. "Time passes, and when it does, it puts its stamp on us. Our personalities, our dreams. And our faces."

She almost smiled. One of the best things about being involved with an ex-politician was that he always knew the right thing to say. "It's not that I can't handle a few wrinkles. Wrinkles are a rite of passage. I've earned each and every line. But jowls? I'm beginning to look like a bulldog. Worse. I look like my grandmother."

With both hands, he brushed her hair back, then held her gaze in the mirror. "You're beautiful."

She didn't know whether to laugh, cry or call him out for being a liar. Except he wasn't lying. His voice was husky, his eyes dark with desire. She knew if she stepped back, if she brushed against him, his body would be tight with arousal.

She wasn't beautiful, had never needed to be. But Al thought she was. To him, she was a sexy, desirable, strong woman.

Nothing could be further from the truth. She wasn't strong. She was a coward. Worse than that, she was a liar. Had been lying to everyone for weeks now. Al deserved so much more than her evasions.

He deserved so much better than what she had to offer. She just hoped he didn't realize it. That she didn't lose him.

She met his hazel eyes in the mirror. "Al, I…I'm not sure I can go through with this," she said, pushing the words out before she lost her nerve. She swallowed, but it still felt as if there was a pebble lodged in her throat. "I'm not sure we should get married."

Taking her by the shoulders, he gently turned her to face him. Searched her eyes. "You want to call off the wedding?" he asked in his smooth voice. There was no anger in his tone, no accusation. Just compassion. He knew how difficult this was for her.

"No. I want to marry you. That's why I hired Yvonne and moved up the date of the wedding. I…I wanted to tie you to me as soon as possible."

"I'm already tied to you. I want to be tied to you. Double knots," he assured her, so somberly she knew it was his poor attempt at humor. He took her hands in his and frowned. "You're freezing. Let's get you dressed, maybe go downstairs, have a glass of wine. Then we can talk this all out."

She *was* cold, her fingers numb with fear. She wanted to go with him. To let him help dress her. To be pampered. For once, she wanted to be taken care of. But that would be the easy way out and she couldn't do that. Not any longer.

When he let got of her hands and bent to pick up her forgotten towel, she grabbed hold of him again, her fingers tight on his wrists. "I'm scared," she told him, her voice barely above a whisper.

"Of marrying me?"

"Partly. I don't want you to regret marrying me. I don't want to trap you into something, into a life you didn't expect."

"I know exactly what I'm getting into," he said. "I want to be your husband, for us to live the rest of our lives together. You are what I want."

"I want you, too. So much." With her eyes on his, she slowly raised his hand to her right breast.

His gaze heated and lowered to the sight of his hand on her, his fingers twitching against her skin. Before, she would've pressed more fully into his hand, demanding more of his touch. Now, she moved his hand down. He jerked his eyes back to hers, the desire in them replaced by confusion. Then realization. And fear.

"I'm sure it's nothing," he said gruffly, as if saying it and meaning it would make it true. He kept his hand on her, his touch gentle but firm, as if he was searching for something, anything that would reassure him. Or maybe, as she'd done when she'd first discovered it, he was trying to convince himself that the lump on the underside of her breast didn't really exist. "When did you first notice it?"

She wrapped the damp towel around herself. "Three weeks ago."

"You've known for three weeks and you didn't say anything?" he asked incredulously. "Tell me you've seen a doctor. Or at least made an appointment."

She hugged her arms around herself, but still felt as if she'd never get warm again. "I couldn't," she admitted hoarsely, her shame at her own weakness threatening to overwhelm her. "I'm too afraid. I don't think I can handle them telling me it's…"

God, she couldn't even say it.

"You'll handle it," he said, crossing to the night-stand and picking up his cell phone. He waved it at her. "You can handle anything. You're the strongest woman I know." He put on his reading glasses and searched for something on his phone.

"What are you doing?"

"Calling the president of Georgetown University Hospital." Al pressed a button, then held the phone to his ear.

"But it's after ten."

"I don't care how late—Erin," he said into the phone. "It's Senator Allen Wallace."

While he spoke to the other woman, Diane went to the dresser and pulled a silk nightgown over her head before dragging a brush roughly through her damp hair. If any of her sons saw Al taking over, and her letting him, they wouldn't believe it. She was having a hard time believing it herself. It was such a relief.

The brush got stuck on a tangle. Her eyes watered as she pressed the bristles against her scalp and pulled it through the knotted hair. She used to think she could take on the world and come out on top. Barely nine years ago she'd had her future mapped out as clearly as Aidan mapped out the vineyards. She'd been positive Tom and Matt would eventually reconcile, that Brady would come back from Afghanistan whole and that Aidan and his young bride would decide they'd had enough of Savannah and want to settle down closer to his family. At least one of her sons, she was sure, would come to his senses and take over the Diamond Dust. Until that happened, she and Tom would run it together.

She'd had everything.

Then Tom had gotten sick. And when he died, she hadn't been able to face that future without him. There were so many days she wasn't sure she wanted to face it alone. She'd learned what type of person she truly was. The type who would let one son give up his own dreams in order to keep his father's business running, and threaten to kick another son off her property if he didn't get the help she wanted him to have. Someone who would manipulate and blackmail a third son into becoming a part of that company.

She wasn't as strong as she'd always prided herself in being. The realization was humiliating. Infuriating. And so very humbling.

"Erin's going to look into getting you an appointment, but it won't be until Friday," Al said as he clicked off his phone. "We'll head up to D.C. tomorrow."

Diane's stomach pitched but she nodded. "We'll leave after lunch."

"You'll tell your sons."

It wasn't a request. Unfortunately, she'd never been one to take orders well. "I'll tell them after we know what we're dealing with."

Al's expression darkened. "Diane…"

"No sense in worrying them unnecessarily." With her lips pressed together, she set down the brush carefully instead of heaving it across the room like she wanted. "Weren't you the one who said it was probably nothing anyway?"

He didn't even blink at her obstinancy. "I'm going with you to your appointment. I'll be with you every step of the way."

He knew her so well. Understood that she couldn't admit how much she wanted him there. Needed him.

She hadn't the faintest idea how she'd been so lucky to experience such a strong love a second time. But she'd do all she could to enjoy and appreciate that love in every minute she had left.

She cupped his handsome face, his whiskers scratching her fingers. "Make love to me, Al," she whispered. "Please make love to me."

His gaze serious, he searched her face. "Are you sure?"

Once again she placed his palm on her breast, then laid her hand over his. "I'm sure."

CHAPTER FIVE

"FUNNY HOW I keep seeing this particular side of you."

Leaning into the backseat of her car, her butt sticking out the door as she reached for a binder that had slid onto the floor, Yvonne reared up and rapped her head against the top of the door frame. Tears of pain stung her eyes.

Tossing the binder onto the seat, she straightened and glared at Aidan, though it probably had no effect, since she was wearing sunglasses. Then again, she doubted it would've had any effect without them, either. "Yes. That is quite funny."

Hilarious, really, that he'd sneaked up on her twice while she was in a vulnerable position.

He rocked back on his heels, the sun highlighting the gold in his short hair.

"I'm sure Tony and Terry appreciated the view, too." Aidan nodded to her right, where two men sat on the tailgate of a pickup eating lunch. The one with a beard grinned and waved before going back to his sandwich. The other man, older and a lot heavier, lifted a thermos in salute.

Blushing, she smiled weakly, then turned back to the car. "I take it Tony and…"

"Terry."

"Yes, Terry. They're employees of yours?"

"They work for the Diamond Dust."

She raised her eyebrows. "Is there a difference?"

"For the time being."

She had no idea what Aidan meant by that. And as it wasn't any of her business, she wasn't going to try and figure it out. But he was watching her, his expression unreadable. It made her nervous. He made her nervous.

Always had.

"I have a lunch appointment with your mother," she said.

"Is that so?"

"Yes." She gritted her teeth. "That is so."

Because she had no other choice, she once again reached into her car for the items she needed for her meeting. Her purse and laptop, several bulky binders and two large posters she'd used to make inspiration boards. Struggling to carry it all, and flustered that Aidan was witnessing her doing so, she used her hip to shut the door. Shook her hair out of her eyes.

"If you'll excuse me?" she asked before walking away, her legs unsteady.

Her purse slid from her shoulder to hang heavily on her elbow.

Aidan came up beside her, sighed heavily and took the binders.

"You don't have to do that," she said as she hurried after him.

He didn't so much as slow down. "Consider it my good deed for the day."

Though he sounded less than pleased to be playing Good Samaritan, she wasn't about to argue with him. Especially since those binders were awfully heavy.

He was so quick across the cement driveway, she soon lagged behind, unwilling to scurry after him in her heels. She glanced at his back, the broad line of his shoulders, the sliver of skin visible at the nape of his neck. Her fingers twitched. She knew what that skin felt like. How soft it was. How much he liked to be touched there. Kissed there.

Warmth suffused her and she yanked her gaze up to the Sheppards' large, plantation-style house. To distract herself, she took inventory: two stories, wide porches on both the ground and upper level, a dozen tall, narrow windows, black shutters and a deep blue front door surrounded by leaded glass. It was intimidating. Like its sole occupant.

Still, the small additions of a twiglike wreath on the door, a wooden swing on the porch and gauzy curtains hanging in the lower windows gave the house a warm, welcoming feel.

Except no matter what Diane said, Yvonne knew she wasn't welcome.

She caught up with Aidan on the porch. Knew he was waiting for her to get the door but she couldn't make herself go inside. Not yet. "Do you have today off?" she asked.

"Nope."

"Oh. It's just…you don't look like you're working," she heard herself say of his dark jeans and hunter green flannel shirt, his hair sticking up on the side, his cheeks pink from the cool breeze.

"Because I'm not wearing a suit?" he asked in a tone she couldn't decipher. "Or at least a tie?"

She slid her purse strap up to her shoulder. "Because you're all…mussed."

He smiled. It was brief, and if she wasn't mistaken, it only seemed to upset him that he'd done it. But it was a real smile. One that made him look younger. More approachable. And with his hair, his face flushed, it reminded her of how he'd look after they made love. When he used to smile at her as if he couldn't wait to do it again.

"We're pruning."

She frowned. "But…don't you have employees who…work the fields for you?"

"Yes. But this isn't a Fortune 500 company. We all pitch in where we have to."

She went to tuck her hair behind her ear, only to remember she'd worn it back. Feeling like a fool, she lowered her hand. "No. Of course. I didn't mean to imply you weren't capable of physical labor or…or not involved in all aspects of your business."

His jaw tightened. "Maybe if you'd shown even the

slightest interest in my job, you'd know that being president of a small winery means more than sitting behind a desk pushing papers. At least it does to me."

She stiffened. She should walk away. That's what her mother would want her to do. What Aidan expected her to do.

"It's amusing how you expected me to have such an active involvement in your career when you had so little concern for mine."

"What the hell is that supposed to mean?" he asked incredulously. "I asked you to work at the winery, remember?"

How could she forget? Shortly after Tom's death, Aidan had offered her a position taking care of the books. She'd almost accepted it, had been so pathetically eager to be a part of the Diamond Dust. But by then she'd realized that no matter what she did, she would never belong.

Besides, she hadn't wanted to face Aidan's disappointment and her own feelings of not living up to the standards he'd set for her.

"Well, considering how things turned out, I suppose it's for the best I declined your generous offer. And while I appreciate your assistance with my things, I think it's best if I carry my own weight from now on."

She held out her hands, and after a moment, he transferred her things back to her before going inside, leaving the door open after him.

Leaving her standing there, remembering how, to her husband, the person she was hadn't been good enough.

AIDAN STRODE THROUGH the foyer, but stopped before turning the corner to the kitchen when he heard voices coming from the other room. Including Connie's and Matt's and his mother's. He did a few slow neck rolls to ease the tension tightening his shoulders, then did an about-face and took a step back the way he'd come.

No. He wasn't going out there. Just because Yvonne had surprised him with how she'd stood her ground didn't mean she'd changed.

He'd offered her a position at the winery the summer after his father died because he did care about her career. About her. She'd seemed so unhappy with the job she'd had as human resources director at Jewell Hospital.

She'd seemed so unhappy, period.

But she hadn't complained about it. No, she'd distanced herself from him. Went somewhere inside herself that he couldn't get to. The harder he tried to get her to open up to him, to tell him what was bothering her, the further she withdrew. And while he saw their relationship deteriorating right before his eyes, he'd been powerless to stop it.

Then, less than a year after they'd moved to Jewell, eight months after his father died and Aidan had taken over the winery, he'd arrived home to find her packed bags in their foyer.

I no longer want to be married to you.

Maybe he should've gone after her. Should've followed her to Savannah, told her he loved her and didn't want her to go. Or maybe the ending of their marriage had been the right move on her part. Maybe her parents had been right—they'd been too young to get married just six months after they'd met, a few days after Yvonne graduated from the University of South Carolina, where he attended law school....

Yvonne still hadn't come inside. He wondered if she'd decided to skip her lunch meeting with his mom. If she'd figured out yet what lay ahead for her.

Not his problem. He turned the corner into the large family room. It opened up into a spacious kitchen with tile floors, oak cabinets and a granite-topped island. The huge refrigerator, double wall ovens and six-burner stove were stainless steel, as shiny as if they'd never been used. A large table took center stage in the breakfast nook, where light poured in through the three walls of floor-to-ceiling windows.

His mother's domain.

He should've gone up to his office. His mom and Al were at the stove, talking together. Brady was at the table, and Matt was peering into the refrigerator even though, from the looks of it, lunch would be served any minute.

"Where were you?" Connie asked from where she sat next to Brady. "I thought you were right behind us."

They'd all spent the morning pruning the viognier

vines. As Aidan had told Yvonne, when something needed doing at the winery, they all pitched in.

"I got...delayed," he said, heading for the sink to wash his hands.

Yeah. Delayed. By the sight of Yvonne's shapely lower half sticking out of the car. That had always been his problem. He'd been too infatuated with her. Had wanted her too much, almost to the point of distraction. Maybe that's why she'd left him. He dried his hands. Did it matter?

He didn't want to get drawn into conversation, and crossed to sit in one of the armchairs of the family room.

Connie got up from the table and went to sit on the arm beside him. "You okay?"

"Fine," he snapped. Hurt flashed in her blue eyes and she slowly stood. He sighed. "Sorry. I'm fine. Really."

"You sure?" she asked, unconvinced. "Because if some—"

"I'm so sorry to interrupt," Yvonne said as she stepped into the room, her eyes on Diane. "I must've had the wrong time for our meeting."

Everyone stopped talking, all eyes on her.

She cringed only slightly, but he noticed. As always, he was too aware of her.

"Not at all. You're just in time." His mom took a red, ceramic casserole dish from the oven, her cheeks flushed from the heat. The scent of something cheesy filled the air. "Would you grab the salad from the fridge?" she said to Connie, who was staring at Yvonne as if she were the spawn of Satan. "Matt, the dishes. Aidan, silverware. Brady, please slice the bread."

Yvonne stood there holding several large binders, two posters tucked under her arm, her eyes wide in shock. Or panic.

Aidan stood and crossed the room to the silverware drawer. He used to do his best to make Yvonne feel welcome in his family. Had always tried to draw her out of her brittle shell.

He no longer cared to break through it.

"I don't want to interrupt a family meal," she said. "I'm more than happy to reschedule."

"And here I thought you were in a hurry to get started," Aidan said, setting a handful of forks and butter knives on the counter.

She shifted her hold on the binders. They were heavy, he knew, but she made no move to set them down. And he sure as hell wasn't going to take them, not after she'd been so adamant about carrying them herself.

"I am. I meant that I could come back. When you all have finished eating."

His mom put a large spoon into her casserole. "No need to reschedule. You can tell us about your ideas for the wedding over lunch."

Yvonne swallowed.

"What Diane's leaving out," Al said with a wide smile, one Aidan could tell had been practiced to perfection, probably on the campaign trail, "is that every Thursday she and her sons and Connie have lunch together." He dropped his voice conspiratorially as he took the binders and set them on a high-backed stool. "It gives her an excuse to cook for them and have them all together for at least an hour." He held out his hand. "Al Wallace. So you're the young lady planning my wedding."

Yvonne finally set the poster boards on an empty stool and her laptop case on the floor out of the way. "It's such a pleasure to meet you, Senator Wallace." She shook his hand. "I'm Yvonne Delisle."

"Sheppard not a good enough name for her anymore?" Connie asked Aidan in a low whisper.

He didn't take his eyes off his ex-wife. "Obviously not."

"That's everything," his mom said, sounding tired. She brushed hair from her forehead with the back of her hand, and he noticed the dark circles under her eyes. Could it be that a guilty conscience was keeping her awake at night? "Drinks and glasses are already on the dining room table so we can get started. Why don't you go first, Yvonne?"

Yvonne blinked. "Oh, that's…that's not necessary. Y'all go ahead. I'll just wait out here until you're done."

"When I cook," his mom said, the brightness of her voice belying the determined glint in her eyes, "everyone eats." She held out a white plate. "Everyone."

Yvonne met his eyes, beseeching him. She seemed so…lost.

"Maybe Ms. *Delisle* would be more comfortable if someone served her," Aidan said blandly.

"Maybe you'd be more comfortable if you took that stick out of your ass," Matt murmured.

Aidan smirked, making sure Yvonne noticed. That she saw how unaffected he was by her.

She averted her eyes.

"Please," Al said, his hand on her back as he guided her forward, "join us."

YVONNE GRANTED DIANE ONE of her pageant ready smiles. "I'd be delighted to join you all. Thank you so much."

Connie rolled her eyes—and Yvonne wanted to shove a piece of bread up the woman's nose.

Clutching the plate to her chest, she passed Aidan and his brothers, keeping her eyes straight ahead. And don't think she missed the emphasis Aidan had put on her last name with his last little quip. Had he really thought she'd keep his name after they divorced? Why would she when she'd never truly been a Sheppard?

Stepping up to the counter, she helped herself to silverware and a paper napkin, the nape of her neck hot. It seemed business dress at the Diamond Dust was T-shirts and jeans. Except in Matt's case. He wore a T-shirt with cargo shorts—despite the fact that it was barely forty degrees outside.

The weight of her blazer pressed on her shoulders; her shoes pinched her toes. She'd worn her black pantsuit and the red silk top with a draped cowl neckline because she'd wanted to look professional. Confident. Competent.

Instead, she stood out like a frilly china doll in a shop full of Barbies—pretty to look at, but not nearly as much fun to play with.

She pretended great interest in scooping out just the right amount of salad.

"You trying to wish that lettuce onto your plate?" Connie asked from her spot in line behind her.

Yvonne's back went up and she met the other woman's eyes. An easy enough feat, thanks to her shoes adding three inches to her height. "Excuse me?"

"You're staring at it like you're trying to move it with your mind. While the rest of us are waiting—ever so patiently—for you to get moving."

Yes, that image of Connie with food shoved up her nose was more and more appealing.

"I'm so sorry," Yvonne said in a placating tone that would irritate the other woman more than any food fight. Moving toward the end of the counter, she glanced at Connie's plate. "I can see you're very hungry."

Connie helped herself to two thick slices of Italian bread. "And I can see you're not," she said, motioning to the small amount of casserole and salad—minus dressing—on Yvonne's plate.

"Connie," Diane said, "could you show Yvonne to the dining room?"

Yvonne bit her lip to stop from pointing out that

she'd been married to Diane's son. That she'd spent several holidays and many family dinners here. She knew perfectly well where the dining room was.

With a shrug Yvonne took to mean she consented to Diane's request, Connie buttered her bread, then walked away. Yvonne followed.

"Must be tough," Connie said as she reached across the table for one of the bottles of water Diane had put out. "Trying to maintain that beauty queen figure." She bit into her bread. "Unfortunately," she said, speaking around her mouthful, "I have the opposite problem. I eat and eat and just can't gain a pound."

Yvonne studied Connie's slim figure in her snug, faded jeans and maroon T-shirt with You Had Me at Merlot across the front. "Yes. That must be terribly difficult."

Connie's answering grin was more than a bit self-congratulatory. As if she'd won some competition between them.

God, Yvonne hated her.

She frowned. No. That wasn't right. Of course she didn't hate Connie. Nice Southern girls didn't hate anyone.

Senator Wallace followed Matt into the room. Matt sat next to Connie. "Just grab a spot anywhere," the senator told Yvonne kindly as he took his place on Matt's other side.

She tried to return his smile, but couldn't manage it when Aidan and Brady came in. She sat across from the senator, leaving the seat at the head of the table and one to her left open. Without so much as a glance at his brother Brady sat next to her, leaving Aidan at the opposite end of the table.

"Do you want something to drink?" Brady asked her, his tone low and gravelly, as if rusty from overuse. Or not being used enough.

She could've kissed him.

"Water would be fine."

He grabbed two bottles, loosened the cap on one, then handed it to her. The unexpected kindness when she was so nervous, when it was so painfully obvious no one really wanted her there, had her throat constricting.

"Thank you," she whispered. Aidan was watching her, his eyes hooded.

But there was something in his expression. A warning, maybe? As if he was telling her not to get comfortable here, not to expect too much.

Lesson already learned, buddy.

"As promised," Diane said from the head of the table, "here is our guest list." She handed Yvonne a piece of lined paper. "On the bottom is the wording we'd like to use for the invitations."

"Thank you." Yvonne scanned the list. There were two neat columns, in different handwriting, telling her they'd each written their own guests' names. She did a quick calculation. No more than one hundred and fifty. Good. With some planning, she should be able to comfortably seat that many people in the carriage house no problem.

Diane forked up a bite of salad. "Do you have the invitation choices for us to look at?"

"Yes. I found several styles I think will work for you." The guest list had been ripped out of a notebook, leaving one side of the sheet torn and ragged. She folded the paper carefully and tore off the tattered strip, leaving a clean edge. "I also came up with a few ideas for table settings and two color schemes for you to pick from."

She'd learned early on that if people had too many choices, they not only found it more difficult to make a decision, but also questioned their choice after the fact. Then again, she usually spent quite a bit more time with her clients than she had with Diane and Senator Wallace.

"Would you like to bring them in here?" Diane asked.

Yvonne rolled the strip of paper into a ball between her thumb and forefinger. "Excuse me?"

"Your ideas. I'd like to see them."

"Now? I…I mean…wouldn't you prefer to finish eating?"

And give everyone else a chance to go away.

Diane sipped her water. "Al and I are heading up to D.C. right after lunch."

"We'd like to be on the road as soon as possible," the senator added.

"You're leaving?" Yvonne asked before she could

catch herself. And from the surprised looks she was getting, she wasn't the only one who'd noticed how put-out she'd sounded. "I'm sorry, I thought you wanted to discuss your wedding with me."

Wasn't that why she was here, being put through this? Or was this Diane's version of subtle revenge against the woman who'd walked out on her son?

"If you're not comfortable discussing it in front of everyone, we can always do it when I'm back on Monday," Diane said.

Yvonne slowly stabbed a piece of lettuce with her fork, but didn't bring it to her mouth. "Actually," she said, using the complacent tone she employed when dealing with a difficult bride, "with less than two months to prepare for the wedding, we need to make as many decisions as early as possible."

"Then I guess you'd better show me those invitations now," Diane said.

"Of course." She scraped her chair back. "If you all will excuse me?"

"I've got it," Matt said, getting to his feet. "I'm heading out for more bread, anyway. What do you need?"

She didn't have the energy to argue. "The poster boards, please. And the binders," she added, when he reached the doorway. "Oh, and my purse, if it's not too much trouble."

She could do without her laptop, but she needed her BlackBerry for notes.

Senator Wallace stood as well. "I'll give you a hand."

"And here I thought you were determined to carry your own weight from here on in," Aidan said evenly.

"How…sweet of you to remind me."

His lips quirked. So wonderful to know she amused him.

"Seems like bad timing for a trip to D.C.," Aidan told his mother as he leaned back in his chair. "A trip I didn't know about until now. Especially when it's obvious Yvonne needs you here to finalize wedding plans."

Diane added salt to her food, her eyes never lifting from her plate. "Al is the guest speaker at an alumni dinner he asked me to attend with him." She looked at Yvonne. "If there's anything before I come back, you can always call or email me."

"No problem." She already had Diane's contact information. "Addresses to go with this list would be helpful." She gestured to the notebook paper. "And I usually have the response cards sent directly to me. I can email you an update at the end of every week."

"That would be fine," Diane said as the men returned, Al carrying the binders, while Matt had her poster boards under one arm, a small stack of bread in his palm and her purse hanging off his wrist.

Yvonne jumped to her feet to take them. "Thank you so much." She set the boards on her chair, leaning them against the back, before pushing her plate aside to make room for the binders. She straightened and felt pinned to the spot by six expectant gazes.

She inhaled deeply and prepared to put on the show of her life.

CHAPTER SIX

YVONNE BLUSHED FROM head to toe, warmth engulfing her, causing sweat to break out along her hairline. She was so out of her element. She wanted her office. Her things. The big desk she could hide behind, the comfort of being surrounded by familiar objects. Of knowing her coworkers—people who respected her, a few who even liked her—were close by.

Usually she felt relaxed with her clients. Was confident she could give them exactly what they wanted, do whatever it took to make their wedding perfect. Now all she felt was exposed. As if Aidan and his family could see she was a fraud. Someone who worried too much. Who was unsure. Who'd been told she would outgrow her shyness, her unease around people.

She hadn't. It'd been easier to take a cue from her mother and keep people at a distance. To pretend to be someone else. Someone secure in her abilities and her place in the world. She'd thought she could keep it up indefinitely during her marriage, only to discover she couldn't.

"Let me find those invitations," she said, her voice taking on a coolness she didn't feel. She set one binder aside, opened a second, only to realize it wasn't the one she wanted. Her stomach tightened. Where was it? Had she left it in the car?

Wordlessly, Brady picked up the binder marked Sheppard-Wallace Wedding and handed it to her.

Yvonne inclined her head in thanks.

She flipped to the first page and took out the three sample invitations she'd chosen last night. "As you can see," she said, carrying them over to Diane, "I kept things simple in both the design and typesetting. Of course, we can always change the font color based on the color scheme you choose."

While Senator Wallace leaned over to see the invitations, Yvonne went back to her seat and took a long drink of water. She picked up both boards, holding them upright on the table. "After seeing the carriage house, I thought we could go with a rustic wedding theme. I kept the color choices sedate. Brown, dark greens and cream, with accents of either robin's egg blue or dusky rose."

On each board, she'd made collages of photos that incorporated the color scheme and overall feel of the idea. The blue had antique lanterns with candles inside, an old barn with a huge twig wreath hung above the doors, small birds nests with robin's eggs, two bridesmaid dresses and a round, three-tiered white wedding cake with roses on the top layer. The white cake on the rose board had red roses on each of the tiers. The rest of the space was covered with ideas for dresses, centerpieces of plain white ceramic vases filled with twigs from cotton plants and a bouquet of brown orchids and dark red roses with a vintage brooch on the stem wrap.

"Those are both lovely," Diane said, for the first time sounding excited about, or at least interested in, her upcoming nuptials.

"What's up with that shoe?" Connie gestured to the rose board with her fork. "You don't really expect Diane to wear something like that, do you?"

Yvonne glanced at the shoe in question—a satin pump with a four-inch heel, straps that crossed on top of the foot and a rose on the outside ankle. "It's just for color reference," she said. "As are the dresses and the robin's eggs."

Yes, her tone was slightly condescending, but only because she was so nervous. And second-guessing herself and her work. She usually took a few days to put together inspiration boards.

"I do like them both," Diane said, either ignoring Yvonne's breach of manners or not noticing it in the first place. "What do you think, Connie?"

She shrugged. "I guess the blue one's not so bad."

Yvonne's fingers tightened on the boards, creasing the heavy cardboard. "I'm so glad you like one of them," she said, in such a sweet tone, only an idiot would think she was being sincere.

Connie was many things, but stupid wasn't anywhere on the list. "And I'm just as glad that you've returned to the Diamond Dust. Why, I don't know how we'd ever pick out matching colors and buy flowers for a wedding without your superior expertise."

Yvonne's lips twitched and she cleared her throat. No use letting anyone here see she really did have a sense of humor. They already had their own ideas about her. Nothing would change that.

"You know," Matt said, laying his arm on the back of Connie's chair, "if you two were guys, you could just get it over with, go outside and beat the hell out of each other." He nodded toward his brothers. "That's how we resolve most of our disagreements."

"Matthew," Diane said wearily, "stay out of it."

He lifted one shoulder. "Just trying to help."

"Your idea of help would be to dress them in bikinis and have them roll around in a mud pit," Aidan said in clear disgust.

Matt grinned. "Not true. But now that you mention it..." He shot a hopeful look at Connie.

She rolled her eyes and shoved his chest. "Keep dreaming."

"You can count on that. And for the record," he said, lowering his voice, though they could all still hear him, "my money would be on you."

If Yvonne had doubted there was something going on between Connie and the youngest Sheppard brother, those doubts were put to rest when Matt kissed the brunette.

Guess the man Connie had been married to when Yvonne and Aidan were together was out of the picture.

Yet another change she'd been unaware of. Well, she'd chosen to leave.

"We're going to go with these," Diane said, holding up a white invitation with scrollwork on the top right and bottom left corners. "And I agree with Connie about the colors. Let's do the blue and brown." The senator touched the back of Diane's neck, then looked pointedly at his watch. She patted his hand. "That's my cue that we have to be going."

"Oh, but I only have a few more quick questions," Yvonne blurted when they stood. "I need to know if you have any preference for the caterer and florist and—"

"My only preference is that they're local businesses," she said, pushing her chair in. "Aidan can tell you which ones are the best."

Aidan narrowed his eyes. "I can?"

He could?

Diane didn't even blink. "Of course. This isn't just about our wedding. It's also about the Diamond Dust."

"And God knows you're all about this place," Matt muttered earning himself a cuff upside the head from Connie.

"You're an idiot," said Brady.

Aidan shifted his gaze back to his mother. "You're about as subtle as a brick to the head."

"I don't have time to be subtle," Diane snapped. Al laid his hand on her lower back and she inhaled deeply. "It's less than a month and a half until our wedding. And we have Yvonne here for only a short time to help us move into events hosting. We need to take action on both now. Which is why," she said to Yvonne, "I'd like you and Connie to get started on the bigger-picture steps."

"Connie?" She hadn't asked who, exactly, she was to be working with. She'd assumed it would be someone new, someone with at least a background in event hosting. Someone who didn't dislike her so much.

"Connie's going to be in charge of events at the winery," Aidan said. Connie looked less than thrilled. "But all decisions made have to go through me first."

"Yes," Yvonne said. "Your mother mentioned that. We really do need to make some decisions, Connie, especially in coming up with companies we—I mean, you all—" she glanced around the table "—may want to add to a list of preferred vendors." When Connie just stared at her blankly, Yvonne added, "I'm free this afternoon."

Connie laid her fork on her plate. "Aren't you lucky to have so much *you* time? Too bad I'm booked solid."

"I'm sure you can find an hour or two to give to Yvonne," Diane said, her light tone not hiding the fact that she wasn't making a suggestion, but a demand.

Connie looked as if she wanted to disagree, but then Matt said something into her ear. "Fine," she grumbled. "But we'll do it while I'm pruning."

"I'm so looking forward to it," Yvonne said with a toothy smile. "When is good for you?"

"After I'm done eating. Meet me at the northwest corner of the merlot block."

"I'm afraid I left my handy compass in my other purse."

Connie rolled her eyes. "Just meet me in the parking lot behind the winery in fifteen minutes." Her plate in hand, she stood. "I'm going to get seconds."

As she walked out of the room, the senator laid a hand on Diane's shoulder. "We really need to go."

Diane's expression seemed strained. "Let me get the leftovers boxed up," she said, stacking her plate with her fiancé's, "and the dishes in the—"

"I'm sure the boys can handle kitchen duty," Senator Wallace said.

Yvonne pressed her lips together so she wouldn't laugh at Aidan and his brothers being referred to as boys.

"They have their own work—"

"Diane."

Diane looked at him sharply, but set the plates down.

"We've got it," Brady told them.

"Well, then," Diane said, her voice sounding suspiciously thick, as if she was fighting tears. "I'll see you on Monday."

They left as Connie came back in. Moments later, Yvonne realized how quiet the room was. The silence oppressive and expectant. And worse, all eyes were on her. She had no idea what to say next.

"I'd like to thank you," she said in a breathless rush,

"for this opportunity. I'm very excited to be working..." *With you all.* But no matter how hard she tried, she couldn't force the lie past her lips. "...here."

"That's quite understandable," Aidan said.

"Why don't you quit being a jackass?" Matt asked his brother as he gathered the unopened drinks. "There's nothing wrong with looking out for your own best interests."

"You're good at that, Yvonne, aren't you?" Aidan murmured. As she stiffened, he added, "At making things seem perfect, too. Too bad at least one of the events you planned didn't go as smoothly as I'm sure you would've liked."

She had no idea what he was talking about.

"What happened at the Collins-Webster wedding?" he asked. "The unavoidable?"

She went hot, then cold. How had he found out about that?

God, she had to work with these people for the next two months. People she used to care about, who she used to wish would care about her.

And Aidan wanted to humiliate her in front of them. Wanted to hurt her.

She shook her head slightly, but it did no good.

"Because it seems to me," he said, as if they were discussing who would wash the dishes and who would dry, "some things *are* unavoidable. Such as getting caught in a compromising position with one of your clients on the day of his wedding."

THE ROOM WENT SILENT for one heartbeat. Then two. Yvonne's face was pale.

"God, Aidan," Connie whispered, "way to be a major prick."

He didn't so much as glance at her. Couldn't take his eyes from Yvonne. She'd gone so white, for a moment he was afraid she would pass out. Brady nudged her water bottle toward her.

"I'm afraid you've been misinformed," she said, not quite as cool or stiffly polite as she had been.

He got no satisfaction out of that. But he was still unable to stop from saying, "I'm sure we'd all be interested in hearing the real story then."

"I think we've all heard enough." Brady sent Aidan one of his rarely used but highly effective shut-the-hell-up looks. "Yvonne is a member of the Diamond Dust now. What matters is how she performs her job here. Not what happened in the past."

"You're wrong," Aidan said quietly. "The past does matter. It shapes you. Teaches you valuable lessons."

Such as trusting the wrong person. Loving her. Thinking, for even one second, that she could change.

Yvonne slowly, carefully put the invitation his mother had chosen back into the binder. "I'm so sorry, but I just remembered I have a few calls I have to make. I'll meet you at the winery," she said to Connie. "Whenever you're finished, of course." After tucking the posters under her arm, she stacked the binders, then picked them up, hugging them to her chest. She glanced around the table. "If you'll all excuse me?"

And then, a small smile on her face, her curves making what should've been a plain, masculine suit incredibly sexy, she turned and swept out of the room.

"I don't know if I should be in awe of her control," Matt said, "or her acting skills."

"Both," Connie stated, sounding reluctantly impressed. She stabbed a finger in Aidan's direction. "But if it'd been me and you'd brought up something like that, you'd be wearing my lunch on your head."

"I can't be the only one wondering why she agreed to take this job." He leaned forward earnestly. "We have a right to know if something happened that tainted her career or her reputation, especially if it's going to affect the Diamond Dust by her being here."

"Cut the bullshit," Matt said. "We all know what you were really trying to do."

Embarrassed, trying to tell himself he was in the right, Aidan got to his feet. "Then I guess maybe Mom shouldn't have pushed her luck by trying to run two sons' lives."

"Where are you going?" Connie asked.

"Back to work."

She turned in her seat as he passed. "You haven't finished eating. And Diane made chocolate chip cookies."

"I'm not hungry."

He'd stepped into the kitchen when Brady's voice reached him. "I wanted to go over—"

"Send me a damn memo," he called, swiping two cookies off the cooling rack on the counter without even pausing.

"What about the dishes?" This last was from Matt, followed by what sounded like someone smacking him.

Aidan kept walking.

Outside, he crossed to the company pickup he was using for the day. He didn't see Yvonne. Not that he was looking for her. He was just…making an observation.

Tony and Terry were gone, too, more than likely already back to work. They'd only driven in from the fields so they could meet Tony's girlfriend, who was bringing his lunch. Usually, during pruning, they all ate in the vineyard—except on Thursdays when, as Al had explained to Yvonne, the Sheppards and Connie ate at his mother's. Though Aidan would've gladly skipped this particular lunch.

He whistled loudly. A minute later Lily appeared from the back of the house, her tail wagging, her ears back as she ran. He opened the truck door and she leaped onto the seat. He climbed in after her, started the truck and drove down the narrow road through the plantation.

Five minutes later, he pulled into the parking lot by the renovated farmhouse they used as their gift shop. The store was open, but there were only three vehicles in the lot, one a small, red hybrid belonging to Pam, their manager. Before he'd taken over, their retail business had often dropped off during the winter months, but that hadn't been the case since he'd extended their weekday hours until seven.

Behind the shop was the winery, a newer structure built to match the weathered appearance of the farmhouse with a narrow parking area for employees. And in the spot farthest from the building, the spot where Aidan always parked, sat a shiny silver Lexus with North Carolina plates.

Lily pressed her nose against the windshield. "Yeah," Aidan muttered, "I can't believe it, either."

He'd figured after what had happened—after what he'd said—that she'd find some excuse not to meet with Connie.

But she obviously wasn't going anywhere.

He could take the truck down the narrow dirt road that wound around the five acres of merlot vines. Everyone else parked in the field, and most of the time, Aidan did, too. But there were times when he preferred to walk. And this was one of them.

He couldn't think of anything he wanted more than the sun on his head, the cool breeze bringing with it the scent of spring, as he walked off his edginess. His irritation.

He wasn't about to let Yvonne—or the nagging guilt inside him—dictate his actions.

Pulling into a spot two down from her, he glanced

over. She slowly turned her head, then turned back to stare through her windshield at the block of pinot noir.

She had no right to be pissed. She'd lied to him. Left him. And his brothers were wrong. He wasn't trying to disparage her character. He'd discovered information about her that, as her employers, they all had a right to know. If it was true.

His blood simmering, he strangled the steering wheel before forcing his fingers open so he could shut off the ignition and climb out of the truck. He walked around to the tailgate, took a pair of loppers from the bed and slung them over his shoulder, his anger building.

As an image of Yvonne wrapped around some faceless, nameless groom, came to him, he swung the loppers from his shoulder like a baseball player warming up before batting.

He'd been trying to get to the truth, that was all. To figure out why she'd been involved with a client. Her beauty meant she attracted more than her fair share of male interest. And if her face and body didn't entice them, her parents' wealth and social standing would. But she'd never played it loose and easy. Had, more often than not, cut off some poor bastard at the knees with one of her cool, condescending looks.

Of which Aidan had firsthand experience. He'd asked her out three times before she'd accepted.

She could have her pick of eligible men. Rich, successful downtown men who could give her the life she'd wanted so badly. Hell, she'd walked away from their marriage to get it. So what had pushed her to risk her reputation and job by hooking up with a man who was engaged to someone else? Loneliness? Desperation?

Switching the loppers to his other hand, Aidan stuck a pair of pruning shears in his back pocket and slammed the tailgate shut.

Lily sat in a patch of sunlight by the front door of Yvonne's car. He whistled. She leaped to her feet, glanced his way, then turned back to the car.

Shit. All he wanted was fifteen minutes where he could clear his head and pretend nothing bothered him. Was that too much to ask?

Apparently.

"What've you got there, girl?" he asked, crossing to his dog. Yvonne didn't so much as glance his way.

He tapped on the window. Still nothing. He would've wondered if she was breathing if he couldn't clearly see her chest rising and falling, her hands gripping the steering wheel.

Probably pretending it was his neck.

Finally, she turned on the ignition and rolled the window down. Raised her eyebrows at his loppers. "Come to finish me off?"

He swung the tool down to his side. "Violence was never my style."

"No," she said softly, "you prefer cutting people down to size with words."

"The truth hurts."

"Is that why you stopped over? To spout clichés at me?"

"No, ma'am. I just came to get my dog." He snapped his fingers and Lily padded to him. "Come on, girl."

He made it as far as the back of her car before Yvonne called out, "Wait."

He turned, crossed his arms. She rolled the window up, shut off the engine and opened the door slowly. Just a crack, barely enough for her to fit through, and as she did, she kept a wary eye on both him and his dog.

Lily barked twice and Yvonne flinched.

"Lily," he commanded, "sit."

She did but her body vibrated with excitement.

Yvonne finally shut the car door. "Thank you," she said, as though forcing the words out. But that was his ex-wife.

Always formal. Always polite.

"You're welcome." He matched her haughty tone. "But I already told you, Lily won't hurt you."

She shaded her eyes with her hand. "I remember."

"Then why do you about jump out of your skin whenever she makes a move or sound?"

Her pretty mouth flattened. "You must be in your glory. How vindicated you must feel, because I'm... nervous around your dog."

"I don't enjoy seeing you afraid, Yvonne."

"No? Just hurting me then. Humiliating me in front of your family."

"That wasn't my intention."

"Please. Don't insult either one of us by denying it."

He stepped forward, but she didn't back up as the old Yvonne would have. She just met his gaze.

"Are you calling me a liar?" he asked softly, trying to pretend he didn't want to pull her to him so he could press his nose against the side of her neck and just breathe her in.

Her throat worked. But when she spoke, her voice was strong. "In this instance? Yes. You must really hate me."

"Is it true?" he asked. "Did you sleep with one of your clients on his wedding day?"

She lowered her eyes. "How did you find out?"

Lily suddenly took off down the road after something. Aidan watched her disappear around the winery. "It's hardly a secret."

"No, it wasn't a secret when it happened over two years ago. But it hadn't been discussed much since then. Which makes me believe you deliberately went looking for dirt you could sling at me."

"Mud," he said, ignoring his embarrassment. "You sling mud. Dig up dirt."

"Ah, but you did both," she said, a breeze blowing a strand of hair in her face. He curled his fingers into his palms so he wouldn't smooth it back.

"I contacted World Class Weddings."

"You spoke with Joelle?" Her hand was anything but steady when she finally slid the errant hair in place.

"It was a reference check." The words came out

rougher than he'd intended. "I do them for all new employees."

"A reference? Really, Aidan, is that the best you can do? And yet you seem so offended that I dared suggest you're not being entirely truthful."

He ground his back teeth together. "Unfortunately," he said, as if she hadn't spoken, "by the time I'd called, the owner of the firm wasn't available. However, the woman who answered the phone—a MaryAnn—was very helpful when I asked about you."

Yvonne smiled thinly. "Oh, I can only imagine how *helpful* MaryAnn was."

Now that he thought about it, the other woman had sounded all too gleeful about filling him in on the details of how Yvonne and the groom had been discovered in the dressing room of the church, while the unsuspecting bride had been two doors down.

"What happened at that wedding, Yvonne?"

She crossed her arms. "I found myself trapped in a very small space with a very drunk groom who thought the best way to handle his unhappiness about marrying his *very* pregnant fiancée would be to make a pass at me. Just as I was about to lift my knee, and hopefully, put to rest any worry of him impregnating anyone ever again, the bride walked in."

Narrowing his eyes, Aidan tossed the loppers onto the ground. "Did he hurt you?" He snatched her wrist and tugged her toward him. "Did he?"

"He embarrassed me. He lied about me and what was

going on, but thankfully, one of the caterers stepped forward. Seemed he'd cornered her in the kitchen. But it wasn't until the maid of honor admitted he'd done the same to her at the rehearsal dinner that the bride realized her Prince Charming was anything but." She tugged, but he didn't loosen his hold. "No. *He* didn't hurt me."

Aidan pressed his lips together.

She was right. He was a liar.

"I apologize," he said with difficulty, his thumb lightly rubbing over her racing pulse before he dropped her hand.

Being this close to her was messing with his mind. Making his body hard. But that was only because she was so beautiful, her features perfect except for the pencil-eraser-size chicken pox scar high up on her left cheek.

It had always been one of his favorite things.

And he couldn't stop himself from tracing his fingertip over it. She stiffened. Her eyes widened. She shouldn't be this…warm, he thought irritably. Or soft.

He trailed his fingers down her cheek. Ran his knuckles across the underside of her jaw. The wind blew that loose hair across his hand.

He couldn't look away from the sight of his dark skin against her pale complexion. His rough hand against the delicate line of her throat.

"Don't," she breathed.

He raised his eyes. "Don't what?"

"Don't kiss me."

CHAPTER SEVEN

Yᴠᴏɴɴᴇ's ᴘᴜʟsᴇ ᴅʀᴜᴍᴍᴇᴅ in her ears. She couldn't move. Aidan stepped closer and it took all she had not to yield to him. His warmth beckoned her to lean in. To trail her hands over his shoulders, his arms, to see if they were as solid as she remembered.

She kept her arms straight at her sides, her palms pressed against her outer thighs.

But she couldn't look away from him. Didn't push past him or move to the side or take the step or two back she needed in order to be able to breathe again.

He bent his head and she stiffened, jerking her own away. He eased back but didn't let go. Oh, no. He slid his hand around to the nape of her neck, his grip firm, his fingers tense in her hair.

"It's not true," he said.

"It doesn't matter," she said desperately, having no idea what he was talking about. All she wanted was for him to stop touching her so gently. Stop looking at her with such hunger. Stop hurting her with his lingering anger and inability to forget their past.

His refusal to forgive her.

"I don't hate you. I wanted to, tried to. This situation

would be easier if I did." His eyes on hers, he lowered his head again slowly, so slowly she had plenty of time to evade. She didn't move. "I can't," he repeated, his breath washing across her lips before his mouth took hers.

She tried to keep her eyes open, her thoughts focused. But he tasted so good, so male and familiar, and he kissed her with an intensity, a passion, that bordered on punishing. Her eyes drifted shut, her fingers curled, her nails scraping her skin through the thin material of her pants.

And, God help her, she kissed him back.

His fingers tightened on her scalp as his tongue swept between her lips to rasp against hers. It was as if she'd been thrust back in time, the years blurring so that she wasn't sure what was real and what was memory.

She didn't want to be sucked into what had been. She couldn't regret leaving him.

Tearing her mouth from his, she pressed against the solid planes of his chest only to snatch her hands back when she felt the strong, steady beat of his heart.

"I'd appreciate..." Because she sounded like a cartoon chipmunk, she stopped and cleared her throat. "I'd appreciate if you wouldn't touch me."

Don't touch me. Don't kiss me. Don't make me remember how things used to be between us.

One side of his mouth quirked. "Anything you say, princess. Anything you want. Isn't that how it goes?"

She bristled. "I have every right to decide whose hands I want on me."

"Absolutely. But let me give you some advice," he said with an all too cocky grin on his all too handsome face. "If you don't want my hands on you—" he lowered his voice as if imparting a secret "—don't kiss me like you do." Then he whistled, said, "Come on, girl," to his damn dog and walked away.

Which was a good thing, since if he'd stayed, she might have slapped him.

She walked back to her car with as much dignity as she could muster. It wasn't until she was sure he wasn't going to look back that she kicked the ground.

Resulting in a scuff mark on her shoe and a sore toe.

And they were both Aidan's fault.

Why had he told his brothers about what had happened with Chad Webster? Now she had to somehow hold her head up and do her job, knowing that the family she'd once so desperately wanted to be a part of were looking down on her.

Unless Aidan told them the truth.

That was doubtful. She wasn't even sure he believed her version of events—no matter that they were the truth.

And now she had to face the fact that she wasn't as over Aidan as she'd tried to convince herself all these years.

As the sound of an engine reached her, she turned to see a white truck barreling down the road. A minute later, Connie pulled into the parking lot—and headed straight toward Yvonne. Or at least, the parking spot where she stood.

She pressed her back against her car, her heart racing as the truck slammed to a stop. The passenger side door opened and Connie leaned over the bucket seat. "Well?"

Exhaust blew into Yvonne's face. She coughed. "Well what?"

"Are you getting in or not?"

"That depends on whether you plan to actually work with me for the promised hour. Or if you're going to leave my lifeless body in the woods where it'll never be found."

Connie's dark blue eyes lit with humor, but her mouth remained serious. "I didn't realize I had a choice. Can I get back to you on that? At least until after I figure out a way to off you without getting any blood on the truck seat. It was just reupholstered."

Yvonne glanced at the ugly brown covering. "Blood may actually be an improvement."

"Look, if the truck's not good enough to haul your fancy ass around, fine. But I'm going to count to ten and then I'm leaving, whether you're in this truck or not."

Yvonne laughed. "I hardly think that's—"

"One," Connie said. "Two."

Yvonne yanked open the door to the backseat of her Lexus, but then hesitated. What should she take?

Connie had said something at lunch about pruning, so obviously they were going into the vineyard.

"Three," Connie said. "Four. Six." Yvonne whirled around to glare at her, and she grinned. "Just seeing if you were paying attention."

Okay, no laptop. With her knee on the backseat, Yvonne reached up front for her keys and sunglasses, tossed them into her purse and backed out of the car. By the time she'd shut her door and climbed into the truck, Connie had reached nine.

"Buckle up," she said, then shifted into reverse and peeled out of the parking lot before Yvonne had clicked her belt into place. "Your hour starts now, by the way."

She didn't slow as they reached the road, but took a hard left that pressed Yvonne up against the door. "I may not live that long," she muttered as they turned off the pavement onto a wide, bumpy dirt road between two rows of brown vines. In case she did survive, she dug her BlackBerry out. "Tell me, what all have you—and by *you,* I mean the Diamond Dust, of course—done as far as event hosting?"

"We—and by *we,* I mean *us*—decided to start offering to host events here."

They passed Aidan and Lily, and Yvonne's heart stopped. Thankfully, Connie didn't offer him a ride.

When her heart resumed its normal pace, Yvonne asked, "That's all?"

"Yep."

She bit back her frustration. "So you haven't done…

anything? Made a list of possible preferred vendors? Scheduled cleanup at the carriage house or looked into any permits or special licenses you may need?"

"No to all of the above. And before you ask any more questions, let me just make it clear that this idea was given the green light only four days ago. One day ago we learned that our schedule for the launch of this venture would be in six weeks."

"Okay." Yvonne cleared her throat and studied her phone's screen. "That's okay. Everything will work out fine." If she repeated it often enough, it was sure to come true, right? "It's…disconcerting…all the work to be done."

She pulled her shoulders back. *It's not the end of the world,* she assured herself. She didn't have much time or—she glanced at Connie—much help to do all the work she'd have to do to make the Diamond Dust the best wedding site in the state. But she'd manage. And her success would be all that much sweeter because it happened here.

Connie pulled to a stop in a field at the end of the rows. There was another white company truck, a black Jeep with a soft top and two four-wheeled, all-terrain vehicles. Without a word, she opened her door and jumped to the ground before reaching back for a faded blue ball cap that was so dusty, Yvonne grimaced when the other woman put it on.

Having no other choice, Yvonne climbed down from the truck, her heels sinking into the damp earth.

Through the tangled branches, she spied people working a few rows away. The quiet was punctuated with an occasional laugh or shout.

At the back of the truck, Connie reached into the bed for a tool exactly like Aidan had carried—it looked like supersize pruning shears—a pair of regular pruners and a hacksaw. She laid them on the open tailgate.

"Here," she said, holding out a pair of worn sneakers.

Yvonne didn't move. "What are those?"

Connie rolled her eyes. "Do you always have to use that prissy tone? Can't you speak like a normal person?"

"I'm so sorry." Yvonne made her accent heavier, her voice prissier. "But this happens to be the only tone I have."

"Lucky for me I get to listen to it, then." She shook the shoes. Specks of mud fell from the soles. "They're sneakers. Trust me, you're going to want to put them on. Unless you don't mind getting mud on those…Choo Choos or whatever they are."

"Actually," she said, admiring one gorgeous pump, "they're Valentino."

"Whoop-de-do." Connie circled a finger in the air.

A bubble of laughter rose in Yvonne's throat. She swallowed it back as she took the proffered sneakers. They were…well…she assumed at one time they'd been white. "Thank you."

Quickly changing shoes, she set her heels in the back of the truck. "And…thank you." She forced out the words. "For what you said to Aidan back at the house."

When she'd called him a prick.

"Oh, hold on, now. Don't get the wrong idea about that."

"And what might that be?"

Connie crossed her arms. "The idea might be that I was sticking up for you or something. Because that's not what that was about. Just because I called him out on being a jerk didn't mean I was doing it for you. I don't even like you."

That admission, so heartfelt, made Yvonne want to smile. "I'm shocked. Truly. You hide your antagonism so well."

"I'm not interested in hiding anything," Connie muttered as she picked up the tools. But Yvonne could've sworn she saw the other woman's lips twitch. "I don't like you and you don't like me. I see no reason to pretend otherwise. And let me tell you another thing—"

"As if I have a choice," Yvonne murmured.

"I'll work with you, but I won't stand by and let you hurt Aidan. Not again."

Yvonne could only stare as Connie flounced away.

Unable to follow, needing to get her emotions under control, she paced the length of the truck, her feet sliding inside the shoes, which were too big. She'd hurt Aidan? Was that honestly what people thought? That her leaving had somehow…what? Crushed him?

More like bruised his ego and his pride.

Because when she'd finally gathered the courage to confront him, to tell him she was leaving, he certainly hadn't acted hurt. More like angry. He'd just stared at her with those cool eyes of his and asked if she was sure leaving was really what she wanted.

When she'd assured him it was, he'd stepped aside and watched her leave.

She'd never regretted it.

And now she was supposed to feel guilty? She didn't believe for one second that her leaving had caused him pain. But she'd suffered, coming to that decision to leave. Had faced doubts during their marriage, spent sleepless nights trying to figure out how to fix what was broken between them. In the end, her only recourse had been to admit they'd made a mistake—that they as a couple were a mistake.

No, walking away from him hadn't been easy.

But it had given her freedom.

THOUGH IT'D BEEN almost half an hour since Aidan had kissed Yvonne, his body was still tense, his frustration threatening to boil over. He could still feel her mouth against his, still taste her surprise, her reaction to him. How her lips had softened and warmed under his, whisking him back in time to when he'd had every right to kiss her, to touch her. When she'd wanted him to.

I'd appreciate if you wouldn't touch me.

He viciously snipped off an old spur from the arm of a vine that had no one-year-old wood. Each of the winery's full-time staff had taken a row, along with one of the seasonal workers they'd brought on a few days ago. Aidan had chosen the row farthest from Connie, figuring he could get through an hour's worth of work even if Yvonne was around. But now he wasn't so sure.

Not when she was still there, typing notes into her phone as Connie continued to prune her vines. Every once in a while Connie would stop to help the new kid, a twenty-year-old from Danville who'd never worked in a vineyard before. She'd also, Aidan had noticed, had to prod the kid more than a few times to stop staring at Yvonne and get back to work.

Wherever Yvonne went, she caused men to act like fools.

Out of the corner of his eye, Aidan saw Matt approach. "I'll take over here," he told Cody, the college worker who'd been with them the past three years. "Why don't you go help Brady? He's two rows over."

Matt took the kid's spot, pulling cut wood that had become tangled in the trellis wire, and tossing it into the middle of the row.

"Brady need help?" Aidan asked, moving on to the next vine.

"He's farther behind than the rest of us but keeping a steady pace. I still think he should be on the tractor."

They trained their vines to a cordon with two arms extending from the main trunk. Out of those arms grew the spurs, and from those, shoots that were now a few feet long. During pruning, they went through and cut back those shoots—one-year-old pieces of wood—leaving two buds on each.

Aidan came to a spot that had two pieces of wood. He cut the thinner one down to the arm and pruned the healthier one. "Driving the tractor's too hard on Brady's knee," he said, not pausing in his work. He'd been doing this since he was ten years old. "We'll let him go another hour, then I'll send him to the gift store to work inventory with Pam."

Brady had come a long way since being injured in Afghanistan almost a year ago, but he still wasn't one hundred percent. He probably never would be.

"So," Matt said, "looks like Yvonne's hour with Connie has been going well."

His cheerful tone set Aidan's teeth on edge. "Looks that way."

"Wonder what they're talking about."

The sun warmed him. A bead of sweat trailed down his spine. "The winery hosting events. What else would they talk about?"

Matt tucked his pruners in his front pocket, then tied a red bandanna around his forehead. "Who knows what women discuss? That's why I asked you."

"You know my favorite part about working with Cody?" Aidan asked. Matt shrugged. "He keeps his mouth shut."

His brother held up his hands. "I just thought you'd like company from a guy who understands what you're going through with Mom and her penchant for sticking her nose into her kids' lives. I've been there, man."

Aidan turned away from the pity in his eyes. "I'm handling it," he said shortly.

"Not very well."

Glancing over his shoulder, he raised an eyebrow. "And you did so much better?"

Lily ran up to them with a stick in her mouth. She dropped it at Matt's feet. He winged it through the air and the dog gave chase. "I had more to lose than you do."

Right. Because Aidan had already given up his own plans, had lost his marriage, while Matt had to decide between chasing after his dreams or staying at the Diamond Dust.

"Seems to me you wound up with the better end of the deal," Aidan said. "As usual."

Matt's eyes narrowed. "What's that supposed to mean?"

"You took off after high school and refused to come back just so you could hold on to your pride and some idiotic, immature grudge against Dad. And yet you still wind up with a full partnership in the winery."

"You left, too. If Dad hadn't got sick, you wouldn't have come back."

"But I did," he said, unable to keep the anger, the resentment from his tone. "It was the right thing to do."

No one had to force him to take care of his responsibilities.

"You're right. I didn't come back willingly. If Mom hadn't threatened to sell the winery and the property if I didn't agree to the partnership, I probably wouldn't have." He cut off an old spur that no longer produced wood. "I can't change the past. None of us can. All we can do is live for today."

Aidan continued working, his movements quick and efficient. "Where'd you come up with that? One of those self-help books?"

"Fortune cookie." Lily trotted back to them and Matt crouched and played tug-of-war with her over the stick. "I might be the last guy you want advice from—"

"There's no *might* be about it. You're the last."

"But you can't hold on to all that anger," Matt continued, as if Aidan hadn't spoken. He'd always been good at ignoring his older brothers. "It'll color every decision you make." He stood and wiped his hands down the front of his jeans before returning to his pruning. "It can even make you act like a complete ass."

"And here I thought that was just your personality."

But Matt didn't give Aidan the fight he was itching for. As usual, his brother never did what he wanted.

"I'm not the one who tried to humiliate a woman in front of our entire family," Matt pointed out.

Aidan snipped at the vine in frustration and almost took a finger off. "I wasn't trying to humiliate anyone."

"That's crap," Matt said cheerily. "But for a minute, we'll pretend it's not. We'll say that you weren't just showering us with the dirt you dug up on her. Why don't you tell me why you did do it then? What are you worried about?"

"I wasn't worried. More like…concerned…about how her reputation would affect the Diamond Dust." He switched the pruners to his other hand, flexed and straightened his fingers. "But I had the facts wrong," he admitted, then quickly filled his brother in on what Yvonne had told him.

"Hell, I can't believe you thought it was true in the first place. I mean, can you honestly picture her having some sleazy affair with a guy who's already spoken for? Or, even more unbelievable, messing around with him at the church on the day of his wedding? All you have to do is look at her, be in her company a few minutes, to see she's not like that."

Damn it, Aidan knew that.

"You're blowing this thing out of proportion and giving Mom the upper hand," Matt commented as he worked. "She's screwing with your life and you're frustrated. Angry. I get that. But it's two months. And the more you fight Yvonne being here, the harder you make it on everyone—including yourself."

Aidan's chest burned. "So I should give in? Reconcile with Yvonne because she's here and Mom wants us back together?"

Staring at him balefully, Matt crossed his arms. "You should stop being an idiot and let Yvonne work. It may not have been the main reason she hired her, and even though you and Connie may hate it, Mom wouldn't have brought Yvonne on board if she didn't think she was the best person for the job."

Aidan stabbed a hand through his hair. "You're right."

Matt shook his head, then tipped it to the side and hit his temple with the heel of his hand. "Sorry. I don't think I caught that. Could you repeat it?"

"No." But he had been right. Their mother was controlling and bossy and wanted to run their lives, but she'd never do anything that would hurt the winery.

"It might help you get through those two months," Matt said, "if you knew exactly what you wanted from Yvonne."

"I want her gone."

"Besides that. Do you want her to suffer? Do you want the next two months to be pure torture for her?"

Did he? And if he did, what the hell kind of person did that make him? "No."

Matt nodded. "Do you want her back in your bed?"

A vision of Yvonne underneath him filled Aidan's mind. Her skin flushed, her eyes glazed with passion as he moved over her, in her. In their bed, the one he still slept on every night, her hair a tangled blond mess, her lips swollen from his kisses. Her mouth parted as she cried out his name.

Shit.

He wiped his hand over his mouth. "Why don't you let me worry about who I do and don't want in my bed?"

"Gladly, as I'm sure any in depth discussion about

your sex life would put me to sleep." Matt's grin faded. "No matter what you decide you want from your ex, it's clear there's unfinished business between you two. If you're not careful, you might fall right into Mom's trap."

CHAPTER EIGHT

FRIDAY NIGHT, WHEN Aidan answered the knock at his door only to find Yvonne on his doorstep, he raised an eyebrow. "Now this is a surprise," he murmured. And not a good one. Then again, in his experience, most surprises weren't.

"Aidan. Hello." Yvonne smiled. That was her, all graciousness and Southern charm. Even after he'd told her if she walked out their front door, not to ever bother coming back. And here she was. "I'm so sorry to bother you at home—"

"And yet you're doing it anyway."

Her smile faltered. Damn it, he'd decided not to let her bother him. To treat her as he would anyone else. But the sight of her standing there, looking like some goddess, undid his best intentions.

She played with the strap of her leather bag, her fingers plucking at it. "I...I do apologize. If you're busy..."

"I have a few minutes," he said. "Although I am curious what you need to discuss that can't wait until Monday when I'm back in the office."

She tucked her hair behind her ear, revealing a small,

gold hoop earring. When his fingers twitched to copy the movement, he curled them into his palm.

"I had a meeting with Samantha Johnson of J & J Floral Design and thought I'd drop off this list of topics you asked for," she said, holding out a manila envelope.

When he made no move to take it, she slowly lowered her arm. "You could've brought it to my office," he pointed out.

"I did," she said, her voice soft in the quiet of the cold evening. "You weren't there this afternoon. And for some reason, every time I call your cell, it goes directly to voice mail."

"Does it?" He leaned against the door frame, making it clear the last thing he wanted was to invite her inside. "Why didn't you just leave the list on my desk?"

"I wanted to make sure you got it." This time she held it out, her hand rock steady, until he took it from her. "I didn't want to arrive for our meeting Monday only to have you claim you never saw it. Unless, of course, you plan on conveniently forgetting about that, as well. Or maybe you'll find yourself called away to prune a vine or watch the wine age or…oh, I don't know…count how many corkscrews you have left in the gift shop."

He didn't even blink. "Are you trying to say something?"

"As usual, you're very astute. What I'm saying is you're avoiding me."

"Now who's astute?"

She shifted from her left leg to her right. "It's certainly your prerogative to ignore one of your *employees,* although I'm confused how you expect me to do my job when I get no support and have no resources at my disposal."

"You have Connie. Didn't she give you more than her initial allotted hour yesterday?"

"Only because it didn't interrupt her work to answer all my questions with single word responses."

He shrugged. "I was under the impression you were the expert when it came to events hosting, and would be guiding us."

"That's what I'm trying to do," she said, though it sounded as if she was speaking through gritted teeth. "And if you could possibly spare ten more minutes, I would love to discuss a few things with you now."

Ever since he'd taken over after his father's death, his mom had been more than happy to step aside and let Aidan be in control. For the first time, he wished she hadn't.

"Then I guess you should come in," he said.

Yvonne hesitated. Then she stepped inside, that damn smile on her face—the one that made him suspect he'd never seen beneath her surface. He backed up far enough to make sure she had plenty of room to enter without so much as brushing against him. She unzipped her jacket, revealing a white, button-down top tucked into the high waist of a narrow black skirt that ended just above the knee.

The outfit should've been sedate. Would have been

if not for her spiked-heel ankle boots, or the flash of creamy skin revealed by the top two buttons of her shirt being left undone. A gold chain disappeared into the V of her breasts.

He shut the door, resisting the urge to hit his forehead against it a few times.

He wished he'd repainted the walls, changed them from the deep slate-gray with white trim she'd chosen all those years ago. He still had the same furniture, pictures and light fixtures. Beneath the window sat the side table they'd bought one weekend at an antique sale. They'd sanded it, then painted it black and when they were done, they'd made love in the shower.

He curled the folder in his hand. He should've changed…something about the house. Anything. Should've hired an interior decorator to come in and wipe away any sign that Yvonne had ever been here.

He made a mental note to do so Monday morning.

"I hope I'm not interrupting your dinner," she said.

"You're not."

"Good. Well," she said brightly, "whatever you're having smells delicious."

"It's chicken cacciatore."

The only dinner he made with any amount of success. And what used to be her favorite meal.

She cleared her throat. "I asked Connie about a time line for the carriage house renovations, but she didn't seem to know anything about it."

"That's probably because there is no time line."

"But you do have a contractor lined up to do the work."

She looked so hopeful, he almost hated to disappoint her. "Afraid not."

"How can that be? Your mother's wedding is in twenty-nine days."

"Not that you're counting, though," he said as he laid the folder on the side table.

"It's my job to count the days," she snapped, then pressed her lips together. He watched as she fought for control. "How am I to plan a wedding when you don't even have a place to hold those events? Or maybe you weren't planning on renovating? Maybe you thought people would want to hold their weddings in a building with no heat, broken windows and no bathrooms."

"Up until a few days ago," he said, crossing his arms, "the whole events thing was just an idea we were kicking around, and my mother's wedding was still four months away, which was why I had planned on hiring someone to handle the renovations within the next month or two. But as soon as the pruning is done—which will by the end of next week—I'll find someone."

"What if you can't? I admit I don't know much about small-town construction businesses, but it seems to me asking a contractor to take on a job that needs to be completed in a month might be out of the realm of possibility."

Aidan shoved up his sleeves. "Your faith in my abilities is heartening."

She blushed, and damn if it didn't make her even more appealing. "Sorry." But then she went right back into professional mode. "Until you do find someone, I was hoping a few workers could help me clean out the carriage house. That way, it'll be ready to move forward when the contractors start."

"I can't spare anyone right now. We're still pruning, and after that we're planting two acres of vines."

"What about hiring someone new, then? Surely you've used part-time workers before."

"We'll be taking on more employees in a few weeks. I'll be sure when that happens, someone can clean out the carriage house."

"Do you want me to fail?"

"Why would I want that? It's my mom's wedding."

Her mouth flattened. "Revenge."

He couldn't help it. He laughed.

"I don't see what's so amusing."

"No, I suppose you wouldn't. This isn't some scheme to get even with you, Yvonne. It's not personal at all. It's business. I have a winery to run—"

"Tell me, Aidan, if your mother's wedding is horrible, will that make you feel better? Will that help you forgive me?"

Do you want her to suffer? Do you want the next two months to be pure torture for her?

"Is that why you accepted the job? You're looking for forgiveness?"

He held his breath, not sure what he wanted her answer to be. Not sure if he was capable of forgiveness.

"I...I don't know." She looked confused. "I did know. A few days ago I would've been able to tell you honestly that the only reason I came back was for my career. But now..."

His heart hammered against his chest. He wanted to step closer to her, to slide a finger down her soft cheek. To remind her of how good it'd been between them.

He didn't move. "But now what?"

She studied him, her dark eyes somber, her mouth serious. "Do you have any idea how difficult it was for me to accept your mother's offer in the first place?" she asked quietly. "To come back here knowing I'd have to face your family. Knowing I'd have to face you again. Can you even imagine what it's like going to work knowing everyone you work with hates you?"

He let out the breath he'd been holding. She didn't want his forgiveness. She didn't regret leaving him. "Poor little princess," he murmured. "Should I feel sorry for you?"

Yvonne realized she was fidgeting, and forced herself to remain still. But it wasn't easy. Aidan was looking at her as if she'd asked the impossible. Plus she was hot. Uncomfortable in her heels and heavy jacket. Out of place.

Her toes hurt. Her heart ached. She wanted to take off her coat, slip off her shoes and feel the coolness of the tile beneath her feet. To stroll through the house, refamiliarizing herself with the rooms.

"When Mom contacted you about taking the job, did she happen to mention my views on the winery going into event hosting?" Aidan asked, his tone giving none of his thoughts away.

Years before, she would've been desperate to know what he was thinking. What he was feeling. But she'd never known how to ask him to share his thoughts.

"Your mother and I just discussed my position and my responsibilities."

"Then I'll explain. The only reason I went along with this whole special events venue was so Connie would stay on at the winery."

"I hadn't realized she'd been considering leaving."

Not that Yvonne could imagine anyone else hiring someone so irritable and hard to get along with.

"It's a long story." And one she obviously wasn't going to get to hear. "Suffice it to say, I believe the main focus of the winery should be making the best high quality wines possible. Anything and everything else is just window dressing."

It all clicked into place. His indifference toward her job wasn't personal. Or perhaps not completely personal. "Maybe if we could sit down," she said, involuntarily stepping closer to him. "I could go over how I envision this. You'll see that one aspect of the business doesn't have to take away from the other."

"I'm not interested in learning anything about throwing parties or planning weddings," he said, his tone making it clear those things were on par with such trivial pursuits as perfecting your golf swing or finding the right shade of lipstick. "And we have plenty of business already. Which means I'm not going to take employees away from jobs that need to be done for something that's not important."

"Like your mother's wedding?" she asked, shocked.

He glanced at his watch. "Excuse me. I need to check my dinner."

He walked past her, cutting through the room they'd used as a dining room to get to the kitchen.

Her hands shaking, her vision taking on a red haze, she followed him—despite pointedly not being invited. He was filling a large pot at the sink. Lily walked over to her, nudged her hand. Yvonne curled her fingers but forced herself not to shrink back.

"So what you're saying," she said, proud of her steady tone, "is that the career I've spent the past five years building isn't important."

That what she wanted wasn't important or good enough. That she wasn't.

Instead of answering, he finished filling the pot. She had a brief—but clear and quite enjoyable—vision of shoving his head under the water and holding it there.

After setting the pot on the stove and lighting the burner, he said, "It's not the Diamond Dust's main focus."

It was even warmer in the kitchen than it had been

in the foyer, the air thick with the smell of tomato sauce and cooked chicken, basil and onions. She shrugged off her jacket and folded it neatly over her arm.

"When do you suppose my *unimportant* job will get some or your attention?" she asked tightly as she went to the other side of the small center island. "How long until you'll have a worker free to clean out the carriage house?"

Shrugging, he leaned against the counter. "A few weeks. Maybe sooner."

"Your mother's wedding is in five weeks and so far the only decisions that have been made are the date and the invitations."

Yvonne glanced around the room. It was so familiar, as if the past eight years had never happened. As if she'd never left. The walls were still a dark cranberry with white trim, the floor a deep walnut, the cabinets oak. Black, high-backed stools matched the glossy black of the counters. At the opposite end of the room a small, square table with high legs sat in front of the large window.

She frowned. The table was covered with a red cloth and two place settings....

"You..." She squeezed the back of a stool. "You're expecting company."

His expression was unreadable. "Yes."

Of course he was. She clamped her lips shut to stop from laughing. It made perfect sense. He was dressed for a date, she realized, in his dark jeans and black sweater, the sleeves pushed up to his elbows, his face clean-shaven. It was a Friday night, after all. And he was a single man. An attractive, intelligent, successful man. He had every right to cook a meal he'd often prepared for her…for another woman. Had every right to bring another woman into their house. To make love to her on his bed.

Had he bought a new one? she wondered numbly. Or was he still sleeping on the bed they used to share?

Oh, God.

She shoved her arms into her coat. "I'm so sorry." Sorry she'd come here and faced the reality of Aidan's life now that she was no longer his wife. Sorry it hurt so much. "I didn't mean to interrupt your evening. I'll see myself out."

Before she broke down. Before he realized what was going on inside her. What she was feeling.

"Wait," he called, but she didn't slow, just rushed through the dining room, past the table that had been given to them as a wedding gift from his grandmother.

Lily must've thought Yvonne wanted to play, because she barked excitedly and raced ahead. But Yvonne's fear of Aidan was greater than her apprehension about the dog, and she nudged her aside with her leg and opened the door.

To see a woman coming up the walk. Yvonne froze.

Aidan came up behind her. "Listen, I'll…I'll see what I can do about getting someone out to the carriage house before the end of the week."

But Yvonne no longer cared about the carriage house or proving herself to the Sheppards. Not when the woman had reached the door, a bakery box in her gloved hand, a smile on her pretty face. She was tall and willowy with glossy, dark, chin-length hair and a dusky complexion that set off the deep green of her eyes.

"Hello," she said, looking at Yvonne curiously, but her expression was warm. Friendly. Yvonne couldn't push out a greeting past the lump in her throat.

The woman looked over Yvonne's shoulder and held up the box. "You said we were having Italian so I picked up some tiramisu."

"Sounds great." His voice was close, his warm breath on Yvonne's ear causing her to shiver.

He didn't even like tiramisu. Or at least, he hadn't when they'd been together.

Things change. People change. Besides, you're not together anymore. The proof of that is standing before you. Standing before you waiting to go through the door you are currently blocking.

Too bad she couldn't seem to move.

Aidan tugged her aside, leaving enough room for the brunette to enter the foyer and shut the door.

Shutting Yvonne inside.

"Marlene Lucca," Aidan continued, as if it was every day his ex-wife and his current…girlfriend? lover? met on his doorstep, "Yvonne Delisle. Yvonne works at the winery."

Nothing. No flash of recognition at the mention of

Yvonne's name. Obviously Aidan hadn't discussed their marriage with Marlene.

She set the dessert box on the side table and then offered Yvonne her hand. "It's nice to meet you. What do you do at the winery?"

"I...actually...I just started," she said, returning Marlene's firm handshake. "I'm the events planner."

"Yvonne is a wedding planner in Charleston," Aidan said as he helped Marlene off with her coat. She smiled affectionately over her shoulder. Yvonne had to look away.

"A wedding planner? That must be interesting."

Yvonne pulled her shoulders back and forced a smile. "It is."

It *was* interesting. And rewarding.

Lily quivered by Marlene's side and she crouched to pet the dog, not the least concerned about getting dog hair on her clothes. Or that the dog might get hungry and suddenly take a chunk out of her person.

"Although Aidan doesn't agree," she said, looking up at Yvonne, "I think the winery expanding into events is a great idea."

"That's because you're all about the bottom line," Aidan said.

Marlene laughed, the sound low and husky and genuine. "I'm an accountant," she explained as she straightened. "So he's right. But bottom line or not, a wedding at the Diamond Dust would be just...beautiful." Grinning at Aidan, she linked her arm with his and pressed against his side.

Yvonne never would've made such a public display of affection, had never been comfortable doing so, not even with such a small, innocent gesture. There had been times, she remembered, numerous times when they'd been out that Aidan had reached for her hand.

And she'd pulled away from him.

He and Marlene looked so right, so perfect together. The other woman fitted here, in this house with her friendly smile, her jeans and ballet flats and red sweater.

While Yvonne had never felt more out of place. More alone.

"Well," she said in an overly bright tone, "I've taken up enough of your time. I'll leave you to your evening."

"Don't rush off on my account," Marlene said, still at Aidan's side, her free hand on his biceps. "If you two have business to discuss, I can keep myself occupied."

"We don't," Aidan said. "We've said all we need to. Isn't that right, Yvonne?"

"Yes. It was lovely to meet you, Marlene. Y'all enjoy your evening."

Quietly, holding together what was left of her dignity, she walked out the door, away from the house she used to call home. Away from the man she used to call husband.

Away from the life she'd thought she'd had no other recourse than to toss aside.

CHAPTER NINE

"IT'S CANCER."

Through the roaring in her head, Diane was vaguely aware of Dr. Pacquin speaking, his voice calm and unemotional. Professional. *Yes,* she thought dully, *we must remain professional. Must remain strong.*

She wanted to throw up.

"Invasive ductal carcinoma," the doctor continued, his fingers laced together on his desk blotter. He was young, around the same age as her sons. How many more people would he sit across from today to give them news that would change their lives forever?

Al squeezed her hand, his palm warm against hers, his fingers strong, his touch reassuring. As if everything would be all right simply because he was next to her. Because he loved her.

Too bad that wasn't how things worked. A fact she knew all too well.

She tried to swallow, but it felt as if her throat was blocked off. It took all she had to drag oxygen into her lungs and blow it back out again.

She sensed her fiancé glance her way. He wanted her to say something, to react to this news. But she couldn't speak. Didn't know how she was supposed to feel or act.

"What do you recommend?" Al asked, leaning forward on one of the leather seats across from the doctor's utilitarian metal desk.

Dr. Pacquin shifted and rubbed a hand over the bald spot at the back of his head. "Chemotherapy, followed by a lumpectomy," he said, reciting treatments as if reading his grocery list, "radiation and hormone therapy. The tumor is just under seven centimeters, so we're looking at a fifty to sixty percent survival rate."

Al's grip tightened, turned almost painful, and Diane blinked, tried to focus. Both men were looking at her, waiting for her to…what? Agree that she was going to be one of the lucky fifty percent who survived? Why should she survive when Tom hadn't?

"I need some air," she blurted. She stood and raced out the door.

She hurried down the corridor. The sterile, antiseptic smell of the hospital only added to her growing nausea. She went past the nurses' station, not slowing when a young R.N. asked if she was all right. With both hands, Diane pushed open the door to the stairwell. The sound of it shutting behind her echoed down the stairs.

She was hot. Sweaty. She pressed her forehead against the cool, gray wall, breathed through her mouth until the churning in her stomach subsided. She slowly rolled her head back and forth. She was sick. She hadn't needed some doctor barely out of med school to tell her what she'd already known ever since discovering that lump.

Al opened the stairwell door, clearly relieved when he spotted her. "Are you all right?" He shook his head and laughed harshly. "I've asked a lot of dumb questions in my life, but that has to be about the dumbest."

Without lifting her head from the wall, said, "You'll get no argument from me."

He held out his arms. "Come here," he said gruffly.

She almost didn't. Didn't want to show any more weaknesses. But she realized he was doing it as much to comfort himself as her, so she stepped forward and let him hold her.

And though she told herself she didn't need to, that she was strong enough on her own, she clung to him.

"You're going to beat this." His hand was unsteady as he stroked her hair. He leaned back and gently cupped her chin between his thumb and forefinger. "You will beat this."

"There are no guarantees." She'd learned that eight years ago when this same damn disease had taken her Tom. And though it was one of the hardest things she'd ever had to do, she had to give Al one more chance. "I'll understand if you want to…postpone the wed—"

"No." His eyes flashed. "I'm not letting you get away that easily."

"Will it be easier after I've lost my hair?" she heard herself ask, emotion clogging her throat. "How are you going to stand being with me, making love with me after…"

After. After the treatments when her hair fell out, her body ravaged by chemo and radiation. When she was so tired she couldn't get out of bed, when her world was reduced to nausea and mouth sores and pain. After the surgery when they took part of her breast.

"I love you," he said, taking her by the shoulders. "You. I love you because you're strong and capable and brave. I love you because of what's inside of you. And that will never change. Never."

Her nose stung, but her eyes were so dry they burned. "I've been so lucky," she said, holding his gaze, "so unbelievably blessed to have been loved by two strong, caring men. To have been given three handsome, wonderful sons. I built a business from the ground up, a business that's thriving and, best of all, will go to my children. Will hopefully someday to to my…my grandchildren as well. Grandchildren I may never see."

"Don't think like that."

"I have to face the truth, all possibilities."

She'd had a good life. A wonderful life. Plenty of days filled with laughter and joy. But there had been hard times, too. The heartache of losing her parents, the soul-numbing grief of burying Tom. For years she'd dealt with the daily fears of having a son fighting a war half a world away, fears that turned into terror when Brady had been injured.

But Brady survived—thank God. And so did she.

She'd survived her husband's illness. Of witnessing cancer ravage his body. Their hopes dashed time and again when each treatment failed. She didn't know if she could go through that again. Not even to save her life.

"Let's go back to Dr. Pacquin's office," Al said in that convincing way he had, as if stumping for votes. "He said he can get you set up with Dr. Stone, the oncologist—"

"I can't."

"Do you want a second opinion? Dr. Pacquin came highly recommended, but if you're unsure about his diagnosis we can find someone else. Someone with more experience."

"No. That's not it." She inhaled shakily. "I want to go home. Now."

Al nodded, his hands slipping down to her elbows. "You want to tell your sons."

Panic threatened to overcome her. "I can't. Not yet."

"They're your sons," he said quietly. "They deserve to know what's going on. They'd want to know."

"And I'll tell them. When the time is right."

"You'll be starting treatments. There is no other time."

Her heart hammered in her chest. "That's just it. I…I'm not sure what—if any—treatments I want to take."

His hands fell back to his sides. "You aren't serious."

"I'm sorry, I know this isn't fair to you. You're scared

for me—I'm scared for me," she admitted, her throat so raw it took all she had to get the words out. "But I want to go home. I need to think about my options."

"The only options are the ones Dr. Pacquin just told us about."

She could see Al's anger and fear in his face, hear it in his voice. "You don't understand. I've witnessed what treating this disease does to people. How much it costs them. I watched Tom suffer from the side effects. Saw how bravely he fought until his strength was depleted, his body racked with pain. And in the end, nothing we did, nothing he went through, was enough."

Al took ahold of her by the arms again and gave her a shake. "Damn it, Diane. This is different. You're not Tom."

"You're right. I'm not as strong as he was. Not nearly as brave. I have no control over this disease but this... deciding what does and doesn't happen next, I can control. Please. I need this time." His hold though his fingers dug into her. "Now, I can go rent a car and drive myself back to Jewell," she said gently. "But I'd very much like it if you took me home."

LATE MONDAY MORNING, Aidan walked past a pile of old cardboard boxes, two full black garbage bags and a rusted out toolbox on his way to the open door of the carriage house. Leaning in the doorway, he raised his eyebrows at the sight of Yvonne studying an antique sign advertising Overalls that Wear Like a Pig's Nose—complete with a picture of aforementioned pig.

"My grandfather swore that sign would be worth millions someday," he said.

She didn't jump, didn't act as if she was in any way surprised to find him watching her. She seemed...resigned.

"He may have been right," she said, lifting the sign by the edges and walking toward him. "But I don't think overalls or pigs are quite the look you'll be going for in here."

Sunlight filtered through the windows, combining with the subtle glow of the hanging lightbulbs to illuminate the dust particles in the air. Yvonne stood before him, the sign in her hands like a shield. Her hair was pulled back and she wore tight, dark jeans and a University of South Carolina sweatshirt that looked very familiar....

He frowned. "Is that my shirt?"

She blinked innocently. "Not anymore." She brushed past him.

He turned to watch as she set the sign next to the toolbox. "Hey," he called. "That sign isn't garbage."

She brushed her hair off her forehead with the back of her hand. "You're more than welcome to go through these piles and take anything of value home with you."

"That's big of you. Letting me keep things that belong to my family and all."

"I texted your mother last night and she gave me the

go-ahead." Yvonne walked back to him, loose strands of hair curling around her face, a streak of mud—or was that oil?—running down the side of her neck, and a cobweb on her shoulder. "Take it up with her."

Impressed despite himself, he sipped his coffee. He followed her back inside. It was cool and smelled of damp earth and dust. The wood floor was warped, the boards swollen from water and age.

She picked up a snow shovel that was leaning against the wall, and something darted out from behind it and across the floor.

Aidan jumped, lifting one leg, then the other like a puppet on a string, his hands flailing. Hot coffee spouted up through the travel mug's lid and landed on his denim work shirt. "Damn," he muttered, his gaze darting left then right. But the mouse had disappeared.

It could be anywhere.

He looked up to see Yvonne staring at him, her eyes wide. "What?" he growled, trying unsuccessfully to wipe his shirt.

She shook her head. "Did you just squeal?"

The back of his neck heated. "I don't squeal. I was surprised. That's all."

"It's just a little mouse. It's more scared of you than you are of it."

"I'm not scared of a mouse. I just…don't like rodents. Especially when they sneak up on me."

She laughed, then slapped her hand over her mouth. "Sorry," she said, her words muffled by her fingers,

"I'm not laughing at you... Well, I guess I am." She lowered her hand, her eyes sparkling. "But only because it's nice to see you're not quite as invicible as you seem."

"I never claimed to be perfect," he groused, setting the cup on a windowsill. He drummed his fingers against his thigh. "And I'm not afraid of mice."

She nodded sagely. "So you said."

"Look, you want to see me in action? Bring a snake in here. I can handle snakes fine."

"That won't be necessary," she said solemnly, but it looked as though she was fighting a grin. Walking over to a pile of plastic pipes, she clapped her hands loudly. Lily barked from outside, then ran in.

"I wasn't talking to you," she said under her breath, making a shooing motion to the dog. Lily tipped her head to the side and barked again before putting her nose to the ground and exploring the building.

"I'm going to pick up this pipe," Yvonne said, nudging it with her foot. "This one right here." Another nudge. "So if there happens to be any rodent-type animals currently living in this pipe, make your presence known."

"I realize a lot can change over the years," Aidan said, "but I never would've guessed one of those changes would be you losing your mind."

Her answer to that was to kick the pipe harder.

"Are you waiting for a mouse to come out and introduce himself?" he asked.

"Don't be ridiculous." She gingerly picked up one

end of the pipe, shook it, then lifted it into her arms. "I was giving any mice that might be living or hiding in this pipe a chance to run off so they don't...surprise you."

Though he felt like an idiot, he grinned. "I've never witnessed anyone being so polite about trying to scare a mouse."

"My mother always says just because you're dealing with rodents doesn't mean you shouldn't be civil," Yvonne intoned in a perfect imitation of Elaine's carefully modulated voice.

He picked up a broom that was leaning against the wall and thumped the bristles on the floor. "I can't imagine that being one of your mother's pearls of wisdom."

"Substitute 'liberal' for rodent," Yvonne said, shifting her hold on the pipe, "and it's a direct quote."

And then she smiled. It wasn't one of her practiced, polite smiles. It was a real smile, slightly crooked. A bit unsure and shy. One that reached her eyes and lit her face. And with her hair a mess and grease down her neck that smile made her seem...approachable. As if there was more to her than her beauty and her family's money, her proper upbringing.

That smile knocked him on his ass.

"What are you doing here?" he snapped.

Her smile faltered and she walked past him, tossing the pipe onto the ground next to the sign. "I'm cleaning," she said as she came back inside.

"I told you I'd have someone clean this place out by the end of the week."

She took hold of his old Huffy's handlebars and, despite the two flat tires, pushed it toward the door. "I needed something to do."

And that's when he saw the stiffness of her shoulders. Heard the trace of irritation in her tone. He stepped into her path, forcing her to stop or mow him over with his own bike. "Did something happen?"

He didn't think she'd tell him, didn't think she wanted to, but then she straightened, letting the bike rest against her thighs. "I'm just…having some trouble finding a decent caterer in town to list as a preferred vendor. But I'll handle it. I mean, there has to be a restaurant or small catering business that doesn't feature fried mozzarella sticks on their menu."

"I like fried mozzarella sticks."

Gripping the handlebars once again, she skirted around him. "Evidently, so does everyone else in Jewell."

That was her job, wasn't it? To find the caterers, florists, musicians…everything that went with getting married. But she was working for him.

Do you want me to fail?

He didn't. But he also didn't want to go out of his way to help see her succeed. Even though his mom had commanded him to.

"I'll get you that list of people to contact," he told her

when she reentered the building, "the one…my mother said to put together."

Yvonne eyed him warily. Good call on her part. "Thank you. That would be very helpful."

He swept the floor in front of his feet. Back and forth. Back and forth. That was him. Mr. Helpful. Mr. You Can Count on Me to Do What's Right.

Mr. Patsy.

He stopped sweeping. "Look, the reason I'm here is—"

"Now, don't tell me," she said serenely, but there was a glint in her eyes that told him she wasn't as calm as she wanted him to believe. "Let me guess." She tapped her index finger against her lower lip. "I know. You're canceling our meeting for this afternoon. Or you're firing me. Again."

When had she gotten to be such a smart-ass? And why did he find it so appealing? "I hired a contractor."

"You… Who? How?"

"Mark Michaels. And the usual way. I called him up and offered him a job."

She looked skeptical. "When can he start?"

Aidan snapped his fingers at Lily, who was digging at the corner of a cardboard box. She hurried over to his side and he patted her head. "Immediately."

"Immed…? Is he any good?"

"Would I have hired him if he wasn't?"

"I can't help but wonder why he can start so fast. Doesn't he have other clients?"

Mark could start because Aidan had promised him a generous bonus. The carpenter had been only too happy to move a few of his other jobs around. "You wanted the renovations started and now they will be." Aidan checked his watch. "Mark should be here any minute to go over the project with you."

"But…but I can't meet him now." She held her arms out. "Look at me."

"He's coming to talk business. He won't care what you're wearing."

"I care." She dived at him—no, not at him, but at the huge bag on the old wine barrel under the window. She tore through it, muttering about men and the importance of first impressions in business relationships.

After taking a small bag out of her purse, she went over to the window, opened a compact and started pressing powder to her face.

Watching her transform herself took Aidan back in time. He'd always been fascinated by her daily rituals when they'd been married. How she'd slather on scented lotions and spend half an hour getting her makeup right, another thirty minutes doing her hair. He'd been so in love with her, so absorbed in everything she'd done. But after a while, he'd grown frustrated with the act.

"Why do you bother with that subterfuge?" he asked when she began to stroke on mascara. "Just for once let the real you show."

Her hand stilled. She slowly put the mascara away

and took out a lipstick. "Who's to say this isn't the real me?"

But it couldn't be. She wasn't this superficial.

She slicked on red lipstick. The shiny color made her mouth seem wider. Her lips fuller.

A car door slammed shut.

With a wince, Yvonne glanced over her shoulder toward the door. She put the makeup back in her bag, yanked the band out of her hair and bent forward, shaking her head. Her sweatshirt slid up, revealing her smooth skin, the slight indentations at the base of her spine.

Aidan couldn't look away.

Flipping her hair back, she straightened just as the contractor walked in, accompanied by a barking Lily. Aidan quieted his dog, but didn't miss the appreciation in the other man's face when he noticed Yvonne.

"Mark," Aidan said, stepping forward to shake his hand. "Thanks for coming. This is Yvonne Delisle. Yvonne, Mark Michaels. He'll be heading up the renovations here."

"Good morning," she said, all sunshine and spring flowers, her hips swaying subtly as she joined them. "It's such a pleasure to meet you, Mr. Michaels." Mark still held her hand. "I'm so pleased you'll be working here. I was worried we wouldn't be able to find someone able to do the job on such notice."

Mark grinned. Aidan was certain he'd have to rip

the man's arm from his shoulder to get him to release Yvonne. "We rearranged a few jobs, put a rush on a couple others."

Yvonne finally tugged free, in a subtle, polite way, of course. "That's very lucky for us. Isn't it, Aidan?"

Yvonne Delisle was putting on quite the show. "Very."

"Well, it wasn't so much lucky," Mark said, "as Aidan's power of persuasion."

"Yes," she said brightly, "I know all about how… persuasive Aidan can be."

He didn't want to know what she'd meant by that. "I have work to do." And if he didn't, he'd be damned if he'd spend any more time than necessary watching Yvonne play Southern belle. "And since I'm sure you have a clear vision of what you want done, why don't you go over the renovation plans with Mark?"

The warmth in her eyes made him think once again that there was a real girl inside her, after all.

"Of course," she said. Then she sent another of those false smiles at Mark, brushing her hair back as she did.

"You can fill me in on the details at our meeting this afternoon," Aidan said, already heading toward the door.

Stepping outside, he glanced back as Mark pointed to an uneven floorboard. "Careful," he said, taking hold of her arm.

As if sensing Aidan watching her, Yvonne looked

over her shoulder and met his eyes for one long heart-beat. And then she turned and did what she did best.

Walked way.

LATER THAT AFTERNOON, Yvonne parked in the empty lot of the Diamond Dust's gift shop. Aidan had texted her an hour earlier telling her to meet him there instead of his office so he could close up the gift shop, since their manager who had to leave early. Which suited Yvonne just fine. She'd never felt comfortable in his father's—in his—office. She wasn't sure even Aidan felt comfortable there. It was as if it wasn't completely his. More like a memorial to Tom.

She grabbed her binder from the passenger seat and climbed out of her car. The bright morning had given way to gray skies and cold, drizzling rain. Ducking her head, she hurried across the paved parking lot and stepped onto the long porch. Not much had changed about the gift shop in seven years. Same weathered exterior and tall windows.

She remembered enough of the family history to know that Tom and Diane had renovated the large farmhouse into the gift shop when they'd started their business. What would it be like, she wondered, to have a marriage like that? A partnership in every sense of the word, where a husband and wife worked together toward common goals. Where they not only accepted their differences, but appreciated them.

Her mouth twisted. She doubted she would ever know.

She stepped inside and let the door shut softly behind her. The floor was a beautiful dark hardwood while a row of wide, rough hewn beams separated the large room. Silver pendant and S-shaped lights hung from the rafters.

"Hello?" she called, slowly making her way toward the back of the store.

Displays were set up on large wine barrels, shelves and long tables covered in green, pink and yellow tablecloths. Along with their award-winning wines, the Diamond Dust carried a variety of merchandise: glasses, specialty food products from the region and an assortment of dinnerware and gift baskets.

Yvonne ran her finger around the rim of a crystal wineglass. No other vehicles were parked outside. Did that mean Aidan wasn't here? She checked her watch. Five o'clock.

"Am I late?" Aidan asked as he walked toward her from the tasting room in the back of the store, carrying a bottle of wine. He'd changed into a white dress shirt, open at the collar.

She touched her neck where she'd rubbed her skin raw to remove the grease. "Yes. I mean…no." As usual, he was right on time. "I just got here."

He set the bottle on a rack and passed her on his way to the door, where he flipped the sign to Closed and locked up. "I looked over the list you gave me Friday night," he said as he walked behind the tall checkout counter. "I'm not convinced we need to invest in tables and chairs this early in the game. At least until we know if hosting events is going to be worth our while. I'd rather rent them."

She blinked. "I guess we're getting right down to business."

Opening the cash drawer, he glanced at her. "Isn't that what this is? A business meeting?"

"Yes. You're right." She straightened her shoulders. "Renting that many tables and chairs is a mistake. Trust me, you'll have no shortage of bookings. I wouldn't be surprised if you recouped your initial investment within a year."

Counting the bills from the drawer, he snorted. "If we do everything on that list of yours, it'll be quite an investment." He jotted down the amount, then tucked the money into a bank bag. "Tables and chairs, sound system, lighting, tableware—"

"It's all necessary." And not nearly the bulk of where the money would be going. "Remember, we're—you all—are starting from the ground up. You had to realize there'd be costs associated with starting a new venture. But by hosting events, you'll increase revenues and brand awareness, bring in more repeat business and draw people here," she said, gesturing to the shop. "All good things."

"It's a little late to be selling me on the idea," he said as he made another notation on a piece of paper. "I'll invest however much it takes to make this a success."

"Good," she said, pulling Mark's estimate from her binder, "then you won't have a problem with this."

Aidan scanned the sheet. "That was fast."

"He seems very easy to work with."

"Why don't I just give the guy a blank check?" Aidan muttered. "Is a veranda even necessary? What's wrong with holding a party out on the grass?"

"We'll have both options. And we can always add the kitchen on at a later date."

He raised an eyebrow. "We?"

She stiffened. "Figure of speech." She'd never been a part of the *we* around here, so there was no need to think that would change now. Even if that had been her initial hope in returning. "I told him he'd have an answer in the morning."

"I'll look this over later tonight and let you know." Aidan counted out some bills and put them back into the drawer. "Was there anything else?"

"No. Not really." And why he was so anxious for their little meeting to be over, she couldn't say. Just as she wasn't sure why she wanted to prolong it. "I got your email," she blurted. The list of florists, caterers, photographers. "I couldn't help but notice a Jane Sheppard. Is that Brady's wife?"

Aidan filled in a bank deposit slip, nodding. "She makes gourmet chocolates. Sold them here during the holidays. We're thinking about making them part of our regular inventory when the baby's older."

Yvonne stared at the back of his head. "They have a baby?" Hadn't she heard they just got married?

"Not yet. J.C.'s due in a few months."

"Oh. That's…nice. I'm sure your mother's thrilled. This being her first grandchild and all."

His hand holding the pen stilled. "Her first grandchild," he said flatly as he began to write again. "She loves Connie's two girls like they were her own granddaughters, though."

Of course she did, Yvonne thought bitterly. She wondered if they'd made room for Brady's new wife in their tight little group, if she measured up to their scrutiny and high standards. Maybe, if Yvonne had given in when Aidan had suggested the time was right for them to have a baby, they would've finally accepted her, as well.

She crossed to a large table displaying hand-painted wineglasses, bowls and serving dishes. "Thank you. For hiring Mark." She picked up a wineglass with brightly colored birthday candles on it.

"I didn't hire Mark for you."

"No, of course not. But I appreciate you convincing Mark to take the job. And, in having enough faith in me to work with him on the renovations."

"Just letting you do your job."

"I…I know you said you'd look over Mark's estimate tonight, but if you'd like…" She swallowed, twisted her fingers together. She'd never, not once, initiated any type of meeting or date with a man before. Not after her mother had drilled into her to always, *always* let the man make the first, second and every move thereafter.

Not when she was terrified of having someone, of having Aidan, turn her down.

"If you'd like," she said, shocked, and yes, impressed by how calm she sounded, how confident, "we could go over them together. Maybe over dinner?"

CHAPTER TEN

AIDAN FLICKED HER a hard glance. "That's not necessary. If I have any questions, I'll discuss them with you tomorrow."

Yvonne tried to convince herself that the only reason she'd asked him to dinner was to prove to them both that she could do so.

"That's fine," she said, as if being shot down didn't bother her. "Whenever." He probably had plans for this evening with the lovely Marlene, who was open and real and wasn't afraid of dogs. "I'll speak with you later, then."

"You and Mark seemed to hit it off," Aidan said before she could leave.

"Yes," she said slowly. "He seems competent. And he had some great ideas for the renovations."

Aidan once again opened the cash drawer, this time taking out the receipts. "That's not the only thing he had ideas about."

"I'm sorry. I don't understand what—"

"You." He shut the cash drawer, slapped the receipts on the counter. "Mark had ideas about you."

Her face heated. "He was very…friendly."

Friendly. Flirtatious. Solicitous. He was also good-looking. Funny. And she hadn't been able to drum up even the slightest interest in him.

Aidan was watching her.

"He invited me out to dinner," she admitted in a rush. "I turned him down."

Aidan's expression didn't change. "That's none of my business. We don't have a policy here against employees becoming personally involved. Although if you were to have a...relationship with someone working for us, I would ask that you do your best to keep your personal and professional lives separate."

His rational tone made her want to scream. "That won't be a problem, since I have no plans to see him other than professionally."

"You're allowed to date him, Yvonne."

She went still. "Thank you," she said icily, "for your permission. But I hadn't realized I needed it."

"You don't. It's been seven years. We've both moved on."

"You certainly have."

She winced. She shouldn't have said that. He'd think she was...hurt by his relationship with Marlene. Angry. Jealous.

Dear Lord, she was all three.

He studied her so intently, she had to force herself not to move when he slowly came out from behind the counter, his gait predatory.

"What did you think would happen after you left?"

he asked. "Was I supposed to sit around, waiting for you to come back?"

"Don't be ridiculous." But she didn't know what she'd thought would happen. Hadn't considered anything other than her need to leave. "You're right. We have both moved on. And Marlene is…" Everything Yvonne wasn't. Everything he'd wanted her to be. "She's lovely. And seems very nice. I…I hope you two are very happy together."

"Do you?" he asked softly. "That's…civil."

She frowned. "Would you prefer I wasn't civil?"

"I'd prefer you were honest. Or is that not possible?"

"I'm an open book," she snapped. "What you see is what you get."

What everyone wanted to see. Who everyone wanted her to be.

"What I saw Friday night was a woman so cold a grape would freeze in her hand."

"I was being polite," she insisted, though his words stung. "I hadn't realized that was a bad thing. Perhaps the next time I run into you and your…and Marlene, I should be nasty."

"At least that would be real." He edged closer. Yvonne stood her ground. "Did you feel anything, seeing me with Marlene?"

Her heart raced. "What do you want me to say, Aidan?"

"The truth. Here, let me show you how it's done." He touched her hair as lightly as a spring breeze, his gentleness in contrast to his hooded eyes, the harsh line of his mouth. "When I heard you'd been engaged, when I saw Mark flirting with you, when I saw you flirting back—"

"I was not flirt—"

"I was…upset."

"You were upset?" she asked incredulously. "My goodness. That certainly was brave of you. Being so honest and all."

His eyes glittered and she worried she'd pushed him too far. "I was pissed," he muttered. "Jealous."

Her mouth went dry. "Is that what you want? Me to be jealous of your relationship with Marlene?"

"I want you to stop giving practiced responses. React. Prove you're human."

No, he wanted her to rip herself open, to give him everything that was inside her while he stood back and judged whether that was enough. Whether she was enough.

She never was.

She tried to brush past him but he blocked her. "Excuse me, but I have a few things—"

"What happened with your engagement?"

"I told you. It didn't work out."

"He cheat on you? Beat you?" Aidan's eyes were narrowed. "Or did you just wake up one day and decide you no longer wanted to be engaged?"

"Is that what you think?" she whispered. "That I

woke up one day and decided I didn't want to be married to you anymore?"

But she wasn't going to explain why she'd left. That would expose too much of herself. It was too late. Besides, nothing had changed between them.

His jaw tightened. "We're talking about your fiancé."

"I didn't love Blake," she said. "And he didn't love me."

"And yet you were engaged to him."

"It seemed like a good idea at the time."

He appeared to be surprised by her sarcasm. "Wasn't your fiancé enough for you anymore? Did you get bored? Or were you waiting for someone better out there?"

"Did I hope there was someone better out there?" she repeated shakily. "Yes, I did. I hoped there was someone who loved me for who I am. Not for what I look like or who my parents are or who someone thinks I should be."

That was all she'd ever wanted. It had just taken her failed marriage and her disastrous engagement for her to realize nobody like that existed.

"Poor little princess," Aidan murmured. "Having trouble finding your Prince Charming."

Her head snapped back as if he'd slapped her. She made to go around him but he stepped in front of her. "Again. I'd like to leave now."

She wouldn't give him the satisfaction of pushing past him or raising her voice, though her throat burned with the need to scream. She wanted to pound against his chest.

He finally moved and she moved past, only to hear him curse under his breath. He caught her by the elbow. "I shouldn't have said that."

His soft tone, the feel of his fingers on her arm, the familiar scent of his aftershave, all combined to undo her. "No. You shouldn't have. But then, you've had no qualms before this of sharing your bad opinion of me, so why start now? You're so arrogant," she said, the words spilling out before she could censor herself. "So superior with your rigid sense of right and wrong. There are no gray areas for the mighty Aidan Sheppard."

Tightening his hold on her, he yanked her to him. She pressed her palms against his chest, and could feel his heart beating strongly. "You left," he growled, lifting her to her toes. "You. Left."

"And you can't forgive me. You want to stay angry, that's your choice. You want to put the failure of our marriage squarely on my shoulders? I'll carry that burden, because I did leave. You want honesty?" she cried hotly. "You want the truth? Leaving you was the hardest thing I've ever done. It was also the best decision of my life."

HER WORDS WERE LIKE a punch in the gut. She didn't regret leaving him. While some days, all he had was regrets.

"Why did you have to come back?" he asked in a

low voice as he pulled her even closer. Her hands were trapped between their chests, her nails digging into his skin. "You should've stayed away."

"I thought you needed me." Her eyes closed, shutting her off as effectively as a brick wall. "I thought your mother, your company, needed me."

The pressure building in his chest threatened to explode. She was always so cool, her facade firmly in place so no one could see past it. She'd never even let *him* see past it. And all he could think of was shaking her until that facade cracked.

"It's always about you. What you want. Your choices." His tone was husky. He couldn't take his eyes from the pulse beating wildly at the base of her neck. "What about what I want?"

"What's that?" she whispered.

He lifted his gaze, met her eyes. They were so dark they were almost black, her lips parted, her cheeks flushed. Her breath washed over his mouth.

She didn't try to twist away or slap or scratch at him. Not Yvonne. She'd never lower herself that way. She just stared at him, her body stiff and unyielding.

He wanted to kiss her. To lose himself in her sweet-smelling skin, her lush curves. Her heat. To pretend she was just another woman, that when she'd left she hadn't taken a piece of him.

"I want to forget you," he told her bluntly.

She nodded. "I want to forget you, too."

Her voice was soft, sad. With his eyes locked on hers,

he slowly lowered his head. She didn't push him, didn't jerk away. Her lips parted.

Sliding his hands up her arms, he cupped her face. And then he kissed her. Kept it controlled, just a faint brush of his mouth against hers. Then another.

All he could think of was being with her.

Except she'd be on her way in less than two months and he'd be damned if he'd let her break his heart before she left this time.

He dropped his arms and eased back. "Now's your chance to make another of your great escapes."

Hurt flashed in the depths of her dark eyes before she turned and made her way to the door, her sneakers silent on the wood floor. But when she reached it, she paused.

"You're so busy blaming me, staying angry at me. Wondering about my broken engagement, my reasons for coming back here. And yet there's one question you've never asked."

"And what's that?"

"Why I left."

THE NEXT SUNDAY, Yvonne climbed out of her car and walked around to the backyard of the Sheppards' house. The sky was overcast, the sun unable to break through the thick clouds, giving the air a chill. She patted her bag, felt the reassuring shape of her umbrella.

Passing the side of the garage, she peeked inside and noticed Diane's boat of a Town Car parked at one end. Though her ex-mother-in-law had been back from Washington for nearly a week, she'd yet to become involved with any wedding plans. Honestly, it was as if the older woman didn't care what flowers she carried or which song was played during the first dance. The other day, Yvonne had had to stop herself from shaking Diane in order to get her to choose between the white butter cake with mocha filling and the almond cake with vanilla filling.

If all her clients were this unconcerned about the most important day of their lives, she'd go crazy.

Not that Yvonne was afraid to make the choices, she assured herself as she stepped around a muddy spot in the yard. But she prided herself on making her brides' dreams come true. And that was impossible to do when the bride refused to participate in her own dream.

Irritated, Yvonne held her breath for the count of five. Her heart rate slowed. Other than Diane's marked lack of interest, everything was going smoothly.

Which, in Yvonne's experience, meant at any minute it would all blow up in her face. She wrinkled her nose. Aidan always used to tell her not to worry so much. To take things as they came. But she preferred planning ahead, seeing the obstacles in front of her so she could avoid them.

When she'd accepted Diane's offer, she'd known it would be difficult being around Aidan so much. That being in Jewell would bring back memories of their shared past. What she hadn't counted on was the attraction between them. She was afraid if she gave in to it, she'd find herself back where she was seven years ago.

Shaking her head to clear it, she turned the corner and scared a robin pecking for food on the hard ground into flight. The best thing was to be strictly professional with Aidan. And she'd found the easiest way to do that was to avoid him as much as possible.

What could she say? Avoidance worked for her.

She hurried toward the back door, barely slowing when she spied Lily lying on the veranda. The dog lifted her head, her tail wagging.

Yvonne frowned. "Uh…hello, Lily." While she knew people talked to their pets all the time, it still felt slightly uncomfortable to be speaking to something that couldn't speak back. "I'll just…scoot around you, if you don't mind."

If the dog did mind, she didn't show it. Just laid her head back down. Yvonne tapped on the door. A moment later, Diane opened it. "What have I told you about knocking?" she asked in a clearly exasperated tone.

Yvonne blinked. "Excuse me?"

"As long as you're coming and going during the day, just let yourself in."

"Right. Sorry." She followed her into the kitchen.

Diane *had* told her that one day last week, when Yvonne stopped in to show her the finished invitations. She just hadn't taken her seriously. And even if she'd thought Diane truly didn't mind people traipsing in and out of her home unannounced, Yvonne couldn't blithely walk into a house where she'd never felt welcome.

But she'd interrupted Diane, she saw now, taking in the metal mixing bowl, utensils, measuring cups, canisters and opened jar of peanut butter on the island. Baked cookies cooled on wire racks, the smell filling the air. Batches ready for the oven were lined up with military precision on baking sheets—three across, four down.

"I'm sorry," Yvonne repeated. "I don't want to bother you."

"Answering the door isn't a bother." Diane's face was pale, her mouth pinched. "It's just easier with so many people coming and going all the time if I don't have to do it."

Feeling unduly chastised, Yvonne stiffened. Would she ever earn this woman's respect? "Of course."

The sound of the television caught her attention and she glanced into the family room. Two young girls with dark hair sat on the floor, a board game between them, their full attention on the cartoon on TV.

"What can I do for you, Yvonne?" Diane asked. She sounded put out, as if she didn't want her there.

She wished the floor would swallow her whole. "I'm meeting Connie," she murmured, twisting her fingers together.

"She's not here."

Yvonne checked the time on her cell phone. "Perhaps I'm a few minutes early."

"No. I mean she's not at the Diamond Dust. She and Matt had to take Connie's mother to the hospital. That's why I have the girls."

The girls who, Yvonne noticed, were now watching her avidly. Yes, she saw Connie in them. The one with glasses had the look of her mother, with her brown hair and sharp features while the smaller one had Connie's dark blue eyes.

Yvonne just hoped for their sake they hadn't inherited their mother's unpleasant disposition.

"I can't believe how old Connie's children are," she said. "She was pregnant with her first one when..."

When Yvonne and Aidan had been married. When she'd left.

"That would be Payton," Diane said with a nod toward the girl with the glasses. "Abby is her younger sister."

They were still studying her. But unlike the stares of adults, theirs held no judgment or expectation. She smiled. "Hello, Payton. Abby. I'm Yvonne. I'm a...co-worker of your mother's."

"Do you want to play Monopoly?" Payton asked, scrambling to her knees. "It's more fun with lots of people."

Yvonne glanced at Diane for help, but the other woman had her back to them as she slid a cookie sheet into the oven.

Yvonne walked toward the girls so she could get a better look at the game board. "Actually, I—"

"She can't," Aidan said as he walked into the room from the hall. His jeans were dark, his deep green sweater bringing out his eyes. "I'm taking Yvonne on a tour of the vineyard."

"You are?" she asked.

"I am." He looked at her in amusement—he'd heard the dismay in her voice. And didn't that make for a promising start to her afternoon? "How about I play with you ladies when I get back?"

"Okay," Payton said with a sharp grin, while Abby ducked her head.

A cell phone on the kitchen island rang. Diane looked at the readout, then wiped her hands on a towel. "I have to take this," she said to Aidan as it rang again. "Could you please wait until the buzzer goes off, then take the cookies out of the oven before you leave? Girls," she called, already walking into the hall, "I'll be right back."

"Can we go outside and play?" Payton asked, but Diane was already gone. The little girl looked to Aidan, who nodded.

Payton had raced out of the room before Abby got to her feet. A moment later, the older girl returned with their coats, one of which she tossed over her sister's head. Once they were dressed and had their shoes on, they ran outside, slamming the door so hard behind them, the walls shook.

Yvonne winced. "They certainly are…rambunctious. But cute," she added quickly, mostly because it was true and only partly so he didn't think she was some evil woman who hated children. "Very cute."

He picked up a cookie and broke it in two. Steam wafted from the center. "I didn't know you liked kids."

She refrained—barely—from rolling her eyes. "Well, it is very annoying how short they all seem to be. Especially the young ones."

"Is that what you're wearing?"

She blinked and then glanced down at her skinny white ankle-length pants, white shirt and narrow belt. "I hadn't realized I was taking a winery tour or that they required a certain dress code."

"We'll be doing quite a bit of walking." He looked pointedly at her black espadrilles.

"These are comfortable. I wear them shopping all the time."

He raised his eyes to the ceiling. "The vineyard isn't a shopping mall."

"On second thought, why don't we just skip the tour today? I'm sure you're busy—"

"I'm always busy," he said, then took a bite of cookie.

Trying to ignore the scent of peanut butter, she swallowed the saliva that had pooled in her mouth. "Which is why I can wait until Connie returns to have a closer look at the facilities."

"I thought you wanted to learn about the winery."

"I did. I do." Yvonne just didn't want to learn from him. She'd managed to steer clear of him for the better part of a week and didn't want to ruin that streak now.

Especially since she was still so confused over that sweet kiss he'd given her in the gift shop. Embarrassed that she'd let so much of the truth slip out.

"If you're sure you don't mind," she said, even to her own ears sounding resigned. "Then I'd appreciate the tour."

"And I'd appreciate if you changed your shoes. I don't want you to twist an ankle."

"That's considerate, but—"

"It's not." He leaned an elbow on the counter. "I don't want any liability issues. Plus if you get hurt out in the vineyards, it'd be up to me to carry your ass back home."

"Your chivalry knows no bounds."

He straightened. "You want chivalrous? I'll drive you to the cottage so you can change. How's that?"

She couldn't help it; she smiled. "My heart is all aflutter."

His lips twitched. "Never let it be said us farm boys don't know how to treat a lady."

And her heart really did flutter. Just a little. But enough to remind her why she fell so hard for Aidan in the first place.

She dropped her gaze. The quiet in the room mocked her. Threatened to overwhelm her. So she reverted to what she knew—small talk. Polite conversation to fill the silence and make it less awkward, at least enough to stop her from feeling so discomfited.

She switched her bag to her other shoulder. Glanced

at the hall where Diane had disappeared. "Do you think your mom's feeling okay? She seemed…" Rude. More brusque than usual. "Out of sorts."

The oven timer buzzed and Aidan shut it off, then used two potholders to take the cookies out. "I think there's something going on between her and Al."

"An argument?"

"More than likely. Things have seemed tense between them ever since they got back from Washington."

"Well, shouldn't you do something?"

Aidan looked at her as if she'd just asked him to bathe with his dog. "What would you suggest?"

"Talk to her. Ask her if everything's all right."

"Sorry. I'm not comfortable getting involved in my mother's love life." He bit into another cookie. "Actually, I'm not comfortable even saying 'my mother's love life.'"

"And here I thought you were the man who took care of everything around here," Yvonne said lightly. "Who solved any and all problems."

And even though she'd been teasing, his expression darkened. "That's me. The original go-to guy." He tossed the rest of his cookie into the garbage. "Except I don't think either one of us should be giving advice when it comes to relationships, do you?"

"Aidan, I didn't mean—"

"Why don't you wait for me out back?" he asked, already walking past her. "I'll let Mom know the girls are outside."

Before Yvonne could answer, he was gone.

She stepped toward the door, only to spin around and grab a cookie still warm from the oven. She ate it in two bites, not caring about crumbs on the floor or that at any moment someone could walk in and catch her in the act. Blushing with guilt and a whole lot of delight, she brushed her hands together and walked outside.

Payton picked up a grimy tennis ball from the brick floor and waved it in the air. "Watch this." *This* was a wobbly throw that arced high in the air before landing with a dull thud in the grass a few hundred feet away. "Okay, Lily. Fetch!"

The dog took off, her dark fur flying, her ears back. She approached the ball at a dead run, only to skid past it before getting her body turned back around, and nipping it from the ground.

"Good girl," Payton said, clapping her hands, her pink jacket unzipped, her dark hair messy—though not quite on a par with her mother's spikes. Lily sat in front of Payton. "Drop it."

The dog dropped the ball at the little girl's feet.

"Very impressive," Yvonne said, while Payton gave Lily's head an affection rub.

She handed the ball to Yvonne. "You try."

"Oh, I don't know…" She glanced behind her, but there was no sign of Aidan. She eyed the ball warily. She so did not want to touch that thing. Not only had most of the fuzz been chewed off, but it was filthy with mud and shiny with dog drool.

Then she saw the challenge in the girl's eyes. Wow. Payton was like her mother in more ways than Yvonne had realized. Poor thing.

"Thank you," she said, using the very tips of her thumb and forefinger to take the ball. "I'd love to give it a try."

Her throw was even worse than Payton's, and went only half the distance. Lily didn't move.

"I guess she doesn't want to play," Yvonne said, oddly disappointed that an animal had shunned her.

Payton rolled her eyes. "You have to tell her to get it."

"Right. Sorry." She looked down at the dog. "Fetch."

Lily took off, got the ball and brought it back. She dropped it at Yvonne's feet.

"Now you pet her and tell her she's a good dog," Payton instructed.

Yvonne recoiled slightly, but Lily stared up at her. She didn't look dangerous, or as if she had any intention of sinking those sharp teeth into any part of Yvonne's body, so she slowly reached out. Lily lifted her head, brushing her nose against Yvonne's fingers.

It was cold. Damp. But she kept on, finally touching the top of the dog's head, her hand unsteady. "Good girl," she said, stroking the surprisingly soft fur.

She heard the door open behind her. "Still have all your fingers?" Aidan asked.

Smiling, petting Lily, Yvonne looked up at him. "So far so good."

Straightening, she noticed Abby standing by the table and chairs, her coat open, her thumb in her mouth.

"Do you want to throw the ball?" she asked the girl. Abby shook her head.

Payton strode over and forced her sister's arm down. "Keep your thumb out of your mouth," she said, sounding so much like Connie that Yvonne shuddered. "Everyone's going to think you're a baby."

Two spots of red appeared on Abby's round cheeks. But as soon as Payton turned back to play with Lily, Abby put the thumb right back where it had been.

Atta girl.

"Come on," Aidan said. "Let's get you to the cottage so you can change—"

"I have flats with me." After she'd had to wear Connie's sneakers in the vineyard, Yvonne had begun carrying a pair of ballet flats in her bag. "I just need two minutes to change."

He looked at her as if the idea of carrying an extra pair of shoes was some new, shocking development. "Why didn't you just say that in the first place?"

"You didn't ask," she said without thinking. But then the words hung between them.

There's one question you've never asked. Why I left.

"If you'd put on the proper shoes in the morning," he said in a tone she couldn't read, "you wouldn't have to haul around such a big bag."

"Thank you so much for that fashion advice."

"Anytime." He leaned toward her and lowered his

voice. "Just don't ask me what I think about how you look in those pants."

She gaped at him.

"Aidan!" Payton called, "Lily won't give me the ball."

Aidan walked into the yard, whistling for his dog.

Reeling from the husky timbre of his voice, the heat in his eyes, Yvonne sat down hard, grinding her teeth together. She glanced at Abby, who hadn't moved. "I don't suppose you know what that was all about?"

The little girl didn't answer. She stared at Yvonne with eyes as deep blue as her mother's. But much less hostile, thank goodness. Yvonne switched shoes, then carefully wrapped her espadrilles in a plastic bag and put them in her shoulder bag. The wind picked up, blowing a dead leaf across the bricks. Abby shivered.

"May I zip your coat?" Yvonne asked, crouching in front of the child. There was no answer. No response whatsoever except for the fluttering of Abby's lashes. Yvonne took that as a yes and pulled the zipper up. "There. Is that better?"

And, miracle of miracles, she nodded.

"Abby!" Payton yelled. "Thumb!"

Abby's face fell as she slowly lowered her hand and curled her thumb into her palm.

"You ready?" Aidan asked as he came up behind Yvonne.

She was too busy digging through her bag to glance

up at him. "Almost," she said absently, pulling out a tube of lipstick.

"Do you always have to hide behind all that makeup?" Aidan asked, so harshly that her gaze flew up to meet his. He looked disappointed. Disappointed in her.

"A woman should always present herself in her best light." As she quoted one of her mother's favorite sayings, Yvonne took the cap off the lipstick and opened her compact.

"Besides," she continued, slicking the color over her bottom lip, making sure Abby had a clear view of what she was doing, "this is the real me." It was all she knew how to be. She held his gaze for one long moment. "Isn't this who you wanted in the first place?" she asked softly.

Before he could deny it, she deliberately turned her back to him. "Would you like me to put some lipstick on you?" she asked Abby.

"She's seven," Aidan said. "She's too young for makeup."

Yvonne kept her attention on Abby's face, knew she had the girl's rapt attention. "It's just for fun."

Finally, Abby nodded and stepped closer.

"Go like this…" She opened her mouth. Abby did the same and Yvonne carefully applied the color. "Okay, now press your lips together. Good. Take a look." She held up her compact so Abby could inspect herself. The girl grinned, her entire face lighting up. "There are two very important things to remember about wearing lipstick," Yvonne began.

"You're kidding," Aidan said flatly.

"The first," she continued, "is to make sure when you apply it, it goes only on your lips—sort of like not coloring outside the lines. The second is even more important. Once you've put all that work into getting your lipstick perfect, you have to be very careful not to do anything that could smudge it, like blowing a bubble with your gum or eating an ice cream cone or…sucking your thumb."

"I won't," Abby said in a sweet voice. She shook her head, her eyes huge. "Not while the lipstick's on."

Aidan laughed and laid his hand on the little girl's head. "You are just like your mother. Always looking for ways to cover your butt."

She smiled up at him and Yvonne's heart lodged in her throat at the sight of the easy affection between them. How…right Aidan looked. How easy it was to imagine him with a child of his own. He'd always wanted children. Maybe with Marlene he could have the future he'd always dreamed of. The big house filled with kids and dogs and a wife who was all the things he needed her to be.

Yvonne viciously tossed the compact and lipstick back into her bag.

"Thank you," Abby said.

"You're very welcome," Yvonne assured her, mimicking her sober tone. Then, as the girl ran off to join her sister, Yvonne turned to Aidan and faked a bright smile. "Well, now, how about that tour?"

CHAPTER ELEVEN

"SHALL I DRIVE MY CAR and meet you at the winery?" Yvonne asked as they walked away from the girls and Lily.

"We're not going to the winery. At least, not first," Aidan said as they rounded the corner of the garage. He'd parked the company's latest investment in the driveway: a cross between a four-wheeled all-terrain vehicle, a dune buggy and a tractor. "And I already have transportation for us."

She glanced from him to the sport utility vehicle to him again. "You can't be serious," she said in that superior way that made him want to throw something. Or yank her against him and kiss her until they were both senseless.

"It's perfectly safe. You'd ride in a golf cart, wouldn't you?"

"Golf carts don't have tires that look like they should be on one of those…creature trucks."

"Creature…" He smiled. "Do you mean monster trucks?"

"Whichever."

He held up his hand. "I promise not to crush any cars or spin any doughnuts while you're with me."

Shaking her head, she crossed her arms, her expression mutinous. "Not. Going. To. Happen. Why don't we take a real truck? One with a frame. And doors that stop people from falling out when going around a curve."

"Because the best way to see the Diamond Dust, to find out what makes it special, is on foot. But," he continued, when she shot him one of her snooty glares, "since you don't have on proper footwear, this is the second best option." He shrugged. "Or you can stop by the gift shop during regular hours and catch one of the tours given to customers. You'll learn the basics of winemaking and they'll even throw in a quick wine tutorial and tasting."

He could practically see her brain working. See how she battled between wanting to refuse him and her desire to get the information he offered. He didn't know why he was pushing it. It'd be easier on him if she joined one of the tours Pam and the women who worked under her at the gift shop gave twice a day during the week and four times on Saturdays.

When they'd been married, Yvonne had shown no interest in his family's business. And while the only reason he was here was because Connie had asked him to pinch-hit for her, he wanted to show Yvonne the Diamond Dust. Wanted her to see it through his eyes.

"Come on," he said, with what he hoped was a charming grin. "Let me show you around my way."

She glanced apprehensively at the utility vehicle again. Bit her lower lip. "I don't know...."

"Why don't you just let loose a little?" he asked, genuinely curious. "Who knows? Maybe you'll even have fun."

Before he could figure out what he'd said to put that hurt in her eyes, she blinked and it was gone. "I know how to have fun," she said, as if he'd just issued an insult. Or a challenge.

And maybe he had. But only because she was so stubborn, so hard to get through to. Only because he was so desperate to prove to himself there was more to her than she let anyone else see.

He offered her his hand. "Then have some fun with me."

Finally, hesitantly, she slipped her hand into his. His chest loosened. Not that her declining would've killed him, but he did like getting his own way.

He helped her into the seat, purposely ignoring how those white pants stretched across her ass as she stepped up. She buckled her seat belt and he crossed around the front of the vehicle to the driver's side, climbed in and started the engine before strapping himself in.

"Here we go," he said, giving her time to brace herself. Then he slowly backed out of the driveway before heading down the road that would take them deeper into the Diamond Dust.

The trees covering the rolling hills surrounding the vineyard were brown except for a few small clusters of deep green pines. Thick, white clouds dotted the blue sky and the sun warmed the air to almost tolerable. Spring was coming. And when it did, his vineyard would come alive again.

Yvonne clutched the handle to her right, her left hand curled into a fist on her lap. "I haven't seen anyone drive this...vehicle before," she said, pitching her voice to be heard over the low engine and the wind. "Do you use it often?"

"Only a few times so far. I ordered it after Brady agreed to work here, around Christmastime. I figured it would be easier on his knee to use this than try to ride one of the four-wheelers or climb in and out of a truck."

"Yes. I...well...I couldn't help but notice his limp."

She was too damned polite to ask what had happened. Aidan stopped in front of the two-story brick farmhouse a hundred yards down the road from his mother's.

"He was injured by an IED—an improvised explosive device—while on patrol in Afghanistan." Aidan squeezed the steering wheel. "He and two of his buddies were injured. A fourth man, a good friend of Brady's, was killed."

Aidan almost jumped out of his seat when Yvonne laid her hand on his leg above his knee. "I'm so sorry. That must've horrible for you all."

He stared straight ahead. Her hand was warm on his thigh. "It was," he admitted slowly, remembering his fear and relief, knowing how close he'd come to losing one of his brothers. "The worst part was he was suffering and there was nothing I could do to help him."

It'd been out of his control.

"You're helping him make a new life," Yvonne said earnestly. "By keeping the winery going, you made sure both Brady and Matt had something to return to. A place to belong."

He snorted. "Except neither one of them wanted to be here. Brady was coerced, while Matt was outright blackmailed."

She straightened, her hand sliding off his leg to return to her lap. He immediately missed the contact. "If I recall correctly," she said softly, "you didn't want to be here, either."

"I don't remember telling you that."

"You didn't tell me. You didn't have to."

Guilt nudged him. He tried to push it aside but it stuck there, just under his breastbone. She was right. He hadn't wanted to drop out of law school, hadn't wanted to give up his own dreams and goals to work at the Diamond Dust.

And he'd never admitted his true feelings about returning. His resentment and anger, his fear of losing his father. He should have.

An apology burned in his throat, but he couldn't get the words out. It was too late for them.

The purring engine vibrated the seats beneath them. The smell of exhaust filled the air.

"Now we're all a part of it," he said. "When Mom retires in July, the three of us are taking over."

"Is that what you want?"

"Of course," he said gruffly.

Yvonne drew back, seemed to shrink into herself. Damn it, he deserved a few hours without feeling guilty for every little thing. An afternoon where he didn't have any responsibilities to anything—to anyone other than himself.

Besides, why should he feel remorse for not letting her inside his head during their marriage, when she'd never let him see the real her? Even now she was pulling her shoulders back, pasting one of those too-bright-to-be-real smiles on her perfect face, getting ready to play a part to get past the awkwardness of this moment.

"What kind of information, exactly, are you looking for from this tour?" he asked.

"I want to know everything," she said, reaching for her purse, which she'd set between her feet. "I need to be able to *sell* the Diamond Dust. I'm hoping to secure a spot for the winery at an upcoming bridal expo in Danville and would like to have some fliers made up of what makes the vineyard special. To do that, I want to have as much information for potential clients as possible. Especially about your family's history here."

"You don't remember?"

She kept her eyes down as she dug through her huge bag. "I'd like to get a fresh perspective."

And that was the best idea he'd heard in a long time.

He could sure use a fresh perspective. "In that case, we have a lot of ground to cover."

An hour later, he drove up a slight incline past a large block of vidal blanc vines. He'd shown her most of the vineyard, had explained how his great-great-great-grandfather William Sheppard had bought this land shortly before the start of the Civil War. And when he'd returned from the fighting, he'd set out to make a living by planting tobacco.

The plantation prospered and William moved his wife and young son from the simple, single-story farmhouse into the grand home where Aidan had been raised. The brick house was built at the turn of the twentieth century to accommodate the growing number of Sheppards. It now housed offices for Connie, Brady and Matt on the first floor, along with a full kitchen. The four bedrooms and two bathrooms on the second floor were used for seasonal workers.

Aidan wasn't sure if it was the story of his family's history here or the fact that he'd kept his speed to a minimum as he'd talked and pointed out the different varieties of grapes they passed. Whatever the reason, Yvonne had long since released the death grip she'd had on the side handle, and she no longer gasped every time he hit a bump. She'd even stopped trying to tame her hair, just let it blow wildly around her flushed face. The wind molded her silky shirt to her breasts.

He jerked his gaze back to the narrow, dirt-packed road. He wanted to stop the vehicle, stab his hands into her thick mass of hair and pull her down to the grass with him. He wanted to see her smile, hear her laugh. Have her look at him with the same heat, the same longing he was feeling for her.

He wanted a second chance.

He bit the inside of his cheek, hard. No, not a second chance. He didn't believe in them. You had one opportunity to make things work, to make the right decision. There was no going back.

"I'm sorry," Yvonne said, and for a moment, he worried that she'd read his mind. But then she held up her phone, which she'd been typing notes into while he talked. "I have to take this call. Could we stop for a moment?"

He pulled over and turned off the engine, then climbed out while she answered her phone. Shoving his hands into his pockets, he strode along the edge of the neatly pruned vines to the top of the hill. From here he could see several blocks of vineyard—cabernet franc, viognier and merlot—as well as the carriage house and the roofline of his mother's place. He breathed in the crisp spring air, held it for as long as his lungs would allow, then exhaled slowly.

Five minutes later, he had his thoughts and feelings under control again as Yvonne hung up and joined him. "Sorry about that," she said, slightly winded from the short walk uphill. She typed something into her phone then slid it into the front pocket of her pants. "One of my brides just found out that her maid of honor broke up with her boyfriend and, as the boyfriend was to take the pictures at the wedding, she's anxious to find another photographer."

"And she called you on a Sunday afternoon?"

The wind blew Yvonne's hair into her face. He curled his fingers into his palms.

"I try to make myself as accessible to my clients as possible," she said. "Sundays, holidays…" She shrugged and smiled. "It's my job."

And from all accounts, one she was good at. At least, according to his mother. Even Yvonne's coworker, the one he'd spoken with who'd been more than happy to share the tale of Yvonne supposedly hooking up with a groom, had grudgingly admitted she was the most requested planner at World Class Weddings.

She'd moved on. As he had. There really was no sense in going back.

"Did you have any other questions about the vineyards?" he asked, more than ready for this tour to end.

"No," she said after a moment. "I think I have everything I need. Except…"

He bit back a sigh. "Except?"

She regarded him seriously. "Do you ever regret it?"

He didn't have to ask what she meant. Did he regret choosing the Diamond Dust over his plans. Did he regret the choices he'd made, the ones that led to their marriage falling apart. He couldn't have any regrets. Refused to.

And yet there's one question you've never asked. Why I left.

"No," he managed to reply. "I have no regrets." He nodded down the hill. "You wanted to know what makes the Diamond Dust special? Well, this is it. It's my family's history. Our future."

"You always wanted so much more."

For over one hundred and fifty years a Sheppard had lived on this land. Woken up to the sun rising over those tree-covered hills. Gone to sleep with the moon casting its glow on the fields as stars dotted the sky.

"I don't know if I wanted something more as much as I wanted something…different. Life in a big city with people streaming all around. An office on the top floor of a building so tall I could almost reach out the window and touch the sun." He shrugged, as if those dreams hadn't been the most important thing in his life. As if giving them up had been easy. "Then Dad died…"

She nodded as if she understood—and he believed she did. "And you were needed here."

"It was more than that. This land is our legacy. This is…it's home."

It was where he was meant to be. Something he wasn't sure he'd even realized until that moment.

"Oh, please," Connie muttered as she looked out of the window above Diane's kitchen sink. "As if she can't get out of Francis without Aidan's assistance."

Diane glanced up to see Aidan help Yvonne down

from the sport utility vehicle—or, as Connie had nick-named it for reasons yet unknown, Francis. "Looks as if at least one of my sons has learned courtesy," Diane said.

"I can hear you," Matt said mildly from where he was sprawled on his back on the family room floor with the girls, playing Monopoly. "And I'll have you know I'm always very courteous. Tell her, Connie."

"Yeah, yeah. You're all gentlemanly manners and whatnot," Connie said. "And this isn't about being polite." She waved the half-peeled potato in her hand. "She's trying to worm her way back into his good graces. I mean...look at her." She punctuated her command by pointing out the window to where Aidan stood in the driveway, the setting sun behind him, his hands in his pockets as he watched Yvonne walk away. "No woman walks with that much...sway...unless she wants to hook a man."

"Sway?" Matt asked as he started to rise. "Where?"

Connie whirled toward him. "Boy-o, you'd better keep your butt on the floor."

Diane's irrepressible son lay back down. "Yes, dear."

"I like Yvonne," Payton said, rolling the dice for her turn. "She's nice."

"And really pretty," Abby added. "She has good lip-stick, too."

Abby had filled all the adults in on how Yvonne had put lipstick on her so she wouldn't suck her thumb. It was even working. Then again, it'd been only an hour and a half. If Diane had to guess, she'd say Abby's thumb would be back in her mouth before the chicken she'd put in the oven finished roasting.

"Yes," Connie said tightly. "Yvonne is very pretty. But there are more important things in life than what you look like."

"Then why do you make me brush my hair every morning?" Payton asked.

"Why, to torture you, of course." Connie went back to peeling potatoes. "What other reason could there possibly be?"

Payton's answer to that was an eye roll worthy of a sixteen-year-old.

Except she wasn't sixteen, Diane thought as she crossed to the door to let a whining Lily outside. Payton was eight and Abby seven. They had so much growing up to do, so many wonderful firsts to experience.

Diane's throat closed. She twisted the rings on her right hand—Tom's rings. Would she be around for any of them? Even if she agreed to the treatment, would she be too sick to make it to Payton's dance recital in a few months? Abby's birthday party in July? Would she be strong enough to hold her first grandson? J.C. wasn't due to deliver until early May. Maybe Diane could put off starting any treatments until after that so she could help with the baby.

So she wouldn't have to face her fears. Her own mortality.

She'd never been a coward before, but now all she

wanted was to stop thinking about what-ifs. Stop worrying about the future, what it held for her, how long she had left on earth, and live in the moment.

Connie and Matt had taken Connie's mentally ill mother to the emergency room for what the attending doctor had diagnosed as a panic attack. They'd driven Margaret home, made sure she had her prescriptions and something to eat, before coming back here to pick up the girls twenty minutes ago. As always, dealing with her mother had left Connie emotionally exhausted so when Diane had invited them to stay for supper, she'd readily agreed—thank God.

Diane didn't want to be alone.

Especially not after the phone conversation she'd had with Al a little while ago. He'd driven back up to D.C. Friday morning to attend a board meeting for one of the nonprofit groups he was affiliated with, and had phoned to let her know he'd set up an appointment for her at the oncologist's office.

He was so worried, she'd had no choice but to promise to keep the appointment. To listen to her treatment options with an open mind.

"I just don't understand why you hired her," Connie said, obviously not done griping about Yvonne. She turned on the water, filling the heavy pot of cubed potatoes. "Is that really what you want for Aidan? Someone so…snobby? So cold? I swear, I get a mild case of frostbite every time I talk to her."

"You're not giving her much of a chance." A headache pulsed behind Diane's temple. "You never gave her a chance. None of us did. We were all too wrapped up in our grief over losing Tom, trying to figure out how to go on without him, how to keep the Diamond Dust running."

To her horror, her voice broke. She turned and crossed to the refrigerator, keeping her back to Connie.

Oh, God, how would her children deal with losing her? She hoped they would stick together, run the winery as they promised, but what if they didn't? Once she was gone, they could break their contract. Go their separate ways.

And what about Al? She stared at the ring on her left hand. Would he forgive her for giving up? Would any of them?

Her mouth set in a stubborn line, Connie placed the pot on the stove and turned on the burner underneath it. "Well, I'm not about to feel bad about how I treated her. She doesn't belong here. She never has."

Diane grabbed an onion and two celery stalks then slammed the refrigerator door shut. "That's not up to you to decide."

"Oh, but it's up to you?" Connie asked, her hands on her hips.

"Yes," she snapped, worried Connie could be right, that she'd made a huge mistake in hiring Yvonne, that Aidan might not forgive her. "I'm his mother. It's *my* family."

Connie pulled her head back as if she'd been slapped.

"Right. Your family. Your company. After all, I'm just an employee."

Diane's stomach churned sickeningly. She reached for Connie, her heart breaking when the younger woman stepped back. "No. Connie, that's…that's not what I meant."

Matt walked into the kitchen. "What's going on?"

They ignored him. "I'd say it's pretty clear where I stand in your eyes," Connie told Diane as she hugged herself. "You made it clear when you didn't tell me about your plan to bring Matt into the winery. But then, why would you? It was family business. And I'm not family." Her eyes welled with tears and she turned to Matt. "I'm sorry, but I can't stay here. Not now. Will you take us home?"

He stroked a hand down her hair. "Of course. Get the girls. I'll meet you in the car."

Diane could only stare, her chest tight, as Connie gathered up her daughters. Payton and Abby must've sensed something big was going on because they didn't argue, just followed her out the door.

No sooner had it shut when Matt turned on her. "What the hell did you say?"

"I…it was a mistake." Her skin was clammy. Cold. She couldn't breathe. Couldn't find enough air to call Connie back, to tell her how much she meant to her. How sorry she was. "She misunderstood…"

But she hadn't. Diane had kept secrets from her. Was

still keeping secrets from all of them. Had put her own wants and needs ahead of the people she loved most.

The door opened and Aidan stormed in, followed by Lily. "What did you do to Connie?" he demanded of Matt, going toe-to-toe with his younger, taller brother. "She wouldn't even talk to me. She's crying!"

With a low growl, Matt pushed past Aidan not bothering to shut the door behind him as he left.

Aidan tossed up his hands. "I give up. What's going on?"

"It's my fault," Diane said, unable to look away from that door, her voice so thin even she could barely make out her words. She cleared her throat. "I said something to Connie I...I shouldn't have." She glanced up at her son. Even scowling he was handsome. All three of her boys were. Handsome. Smart. Kind and funny. And such very good men. "I need to stop them from leaving. I have to tell Connie I'm sorry."

Before it was too late.

But before she got past him, Aidan took ahold of her arm. "Let's back up a min—hey," he said, frowning. "You're shaking. Come on..." He led her to the table. "Sit down. Let me get you a glass of water."

She collapsed in the chair. "I have to talk to Connie. Will you get her for me? Bring her back here?"

He set a tall glass of water in front of her. "Why don't we get you calmed down first? There's plenty of time to talk to Connie later."

Her tears threatened to fall. "But what if there's not?"

SOMETHING ON THE STOVE boiled over, the water splashing and sizzling on the hot grate. Nudging his mother's water glass closer to her, he went to the stove. "What if there's not what?" he asked as he turned down the flame under a pot of rapidly boiling potatoes.

"What if there's not enough time?"

Her voice was soft. His scalp prickled. He began to panic when he turned and saw tears streaming down her face.

His mother was crying. Shit. He glanced around, but of course they were still alone in the room. No one had magically appeared to help him deal with this situation. So he grabbed a napkin from the dispenser and handed it to her as he sat beside her.

"It'll be all right," he said inanely. If it was any other woman, he could muddle his way through. But this was his mother. He was completely over his head here. The only time he'd ever seen her cry was at his father's deathbed. "Whatever happened, we'll fix it," he promised. "We'll get Matt to bring Connie back—"

"That's not it." Diane opened the napkin and patted her face dry. Crumpled it in her hand.

Suddenly, he was glad he was sitting. His legs felt like rubber. "Tell me."

"Aidan, I…I'm sick."

"You're not feeling well?" He jumped to his feet. "What is it? A stomach bug? Do you need me to take you to the E.R.?"

"No. Honey, no." She took hold of his hand, something she hadn't done since he was a child and needed help crossing the street. "I have cancer."

His mind spun. In denial, he turned his hand over and linked his fingers through hers. "If you're not feeling well it could be anything. Let's not jump to conclusions."

She squeezed his hand. "I have a lump in my right breast. Invasive ductal carcinoma."

"Wait, wait." He shoved his free hand through his hair, not willing to let go of her with his other hand. "You already have a diagnosis?"

"Al was able to get me in at Georgetown University Hospital."

"When was this?" Aidan asked suspiciously

"A week ago last Friday."

"You told us all you were attending an alumni dinner," he said, remembering how surprised they'd all been at lunch that day by her sudden decision to head up to D.C. after hiring Yvonne. "You lied to us."

She'd lied to him. He couldn't believe it. She'd always relied on him, turned to him.

She slowly let go of his hand. "I'm sorry. I wasn't ready to tell you. The doctor saw something on the mammogram and was able to fit me in for a core needle biopsy that day." No doubt, Al's influence, Aidan thought. "I didn't want to tell you until I knew what I was dealing with."

"And yet it's been…what? Well over a week since you got the results?"

"Yes. But I'm telling you now."

This was a nightmare. One they'd both lived through before. It had been at this very table where she and his father had held hands and told Aidan about his dad's diagnosis. His treatment options and chances of survival. His parents had seemed so strong. Invincible. And his father had promised to fight with everything he had to beat his cancer. To stay alive.

Aidan linked his hands behind his neck and exhaled heavily. "Okay. Okay." He sat on the edge of the chair. "What are your treatment options? Surgery? On one breast…both? Has the cancer spread?"

She held up a hand. "Dr. Pacquin wants me to meet with an oncologist tomorrow. Al's on his way to get me and we'll drive up in the morning. But I'm looking at six months of chemotherapy, then a lumpectomy."

"So after the chemo, then surgery, then…what? Radiation? More chemo?"

"Radiation but after that, they won't really know what'll be next until the time comes."

He tapped his fingers on the table twice. "You need to tell Brady and Matt."

"I…I can't."

"You mean you won't."

She shook her head. "No. I mean…I can't." Her eyes welled with tears again, but this time she blinked them back. "Aidan, I…I'm so sorry, but I'm not sure I can go through with treatment."

His stomach dropped. "Of course you'll go through with it," he said, speaking through numb lips. "You have to."

"I'm so scared," she admitted hoarsely. "You and I both know that there are no guarantees with cancer treatment. Even with the best care, the best medicine, I could still lose this battle."

Everything inside of him went still and cold. "You won't."

It was inconceivable. He wouldn't lose both parents to this disease. He couldn't.

"Don't do this," he said, not caring that he was begging. "Don't give in without a fight."

"I need some time. And I don't want you to spill one word of this to your brothers."

He felt sick. "You expect me to keep your secret?"

She met his gaze unflinchingly. "I expect you to respect my decision. No matter what it is."

"I'm not sure I can," he admitted. "Not if that decision means you giving up."

"We've been here before. Your brothers haven't. They didn't see your father suffer, what he went through as he fought for his life. I'm just…I'm not ready to face them yet. I can't face them yet." Her voice was thick with unshed tears. "Please, don't tell them. Not yet."

"I won't say anything," he promised gruffly. What
else could he do? He'd never let her down before.

He wouldn't start now.

CHAPTER TWELVE

"You and Aidan looked awfully chummy yesterday."

Yvonne squeezed her eyes shut and said a quick prayer for patience before facing the other woman. "Good morning, Connie," she said. "Can I pour you a cup of coffee?" She held up the pot in her hand with a cheerful grin.

Connie crossed her arms. "I can pour my own, thanks. What's going on between you and Aidan?"

"I'm so sorry," Yvonne said, adding cream to her cup, "but I really don't see how that's any of your business."

"Well, then, let me explain it to you."

Yvonne had just finished meeting with Brady to discuss the text of the brochure she was working on for the upcoming bridal show. She had the finished copy in her purse and had been heading back to her car when she'd been lured into the kitchen by the smell of coffee. And since this was the first time she'd been in the renovated farmhouse, she'd opted to grab a cup and maybe look around.

Sipping her coffee as Connie stalked across the room like a cat ready to pounce, she sincerely wished she'd skipped the caffeine.

Connie stopped in front of her. "It's my business because Aidan and I are friends. Close friends. We've been through a lot together. I picked up the pieces after you walked away."

Yvonne merely lifted an eyebrow. *I have no regrets.* "Whether you and Aidan are *close friends,*" she said, adding air quotes with her fingers for good measure, "is irrelevant. What does or doesn't happen between me and my ex-husband is no one's concern but ours."

With that, she brushed past Connie, fully intending to take her coffee and and get out while she was ahead. And before her bubbling temper boiled over.

"You are some piece of work, you know that?" Connie asked in a low tone. "You think you're something special because your daddy makes boatloads of money."

Yvonne turned back stiffly. "Is that so?"

"Is everything okay in here?" Brady asked from the doorway.

"Stay out of it," Connie snarled, without so much as glancing at him.

"How about I stick around?" he asked in his husky, slow way. "In case one of you needs medical attention."

But Connie just closed the distance between her and Yvonne. Without her heels, Yvonne was a good two inches shorter than Connie, but that didn't stop her from meeting the other woman's gaze.

"You're a spoiled little rich girl," Connie said, "who thinks she can have whatever she wants just because she wants it. Except you already had Aidan, and you were foolish enough to throw him away because Jewell wasn't exciting enough for you, your house wasn't fancy enough. There were no shopping malls or country club dances."

Yvonne set her cup down hard on the kitchen table. She was hot, her silk shirt clung to her lower back, and she felt as if she were about to explode. "You think I left my husband, ended my marriage, because Jewell doesn't have a shopping mall?"

"You were bored. Too good for the likes of a tiny town like this and a man who actually had to work for a living, so you—" Connie flicked her hand "—threw him away. And now you're back because...well, who knows why you're back? Maybe you're lonely. Or you've blown through your daddy's money and need a fast way to make a few bucks."

"I'm back," Yvonne said through gritted teeth, "because Diane called and offered me a job."

"You're trying to worm your way back into Aidan's life, but it's not going to happen. He sees through you now. And if he didn't, there's no way I'd let you hurt him again."

I want you to be real. To prove you're human.

But he didn't see through her. He didn't see her at all. He was just like everyone else.

"You won't let me hurt him again?" Yvonne asked, taking a few steps forward, barely registering that for each step she took, Connie took one back. "As if he even gave a damn the first time." She jabbed a finger at Connie's chest, stopping less than an inch from making contact. "I couldn't stay, but that doesn't mean walking away from him wasn't the hardest thing I've ever done. So don't you dare tell me how hurt *he* was."

A pair of warm hands landed gently on her shoulders. "Let's move back," Brady said as he pulled her away from Connie. "Before you drill a hole in her chest."

Yvonne's body vibrated with anger. "And you know what else?" she said to Connie as she wiggled free of Brady's hold. "You were right the other day—I don't like you. I've never liked you. You're rude and abrasive and selfish."

Connie's eyes widened. "Selfish?"

"You heard me," Yvonne snapped. "When Aidan and I moved to Jewell, all I wanted was to be accepted by his family, to have you all like me. But you were so rude and superior in your place with the Sheppards." Her anger suddenly drained away, leaving only an emptiness in her chest. "I wasn't welcome here." She shook her head. "All I wanted was to belong."

Feeling raw, Yvonne clamped her lips together before she could expose any more truths. She wanted to groan, to curl up in a ball and pretend she hadn't lost control, that she hadn't admitted how much the Sheppards had hurt her.

Instead, she flipped her hair off her shoulder, picked up her coffee and marched out of there as if she was the princess they all believed her to be.

SATURDAY NIGHT YVONNE stepped inside the Empire Bar and Grill and immediately wished she'd stayed at the cottage. Clutching her handbag to her chest, she stood in the archway as the heavy wooden door shut behind her. The building was dimly lit by colored lights hanging from the ceiling, most of them sporting beer names. There was a long bar against the far wall, a pool table to the left and a jukebox in the corner playing some twangy country song.

From what she could tell, most of the establishment's clientele wore jeans and either T's or flannel shirts. The place smelled of beer and whiskey and deep-fried food. And she was as out of place in her dark, designer skinny jeans, flowing silk top and spiked-heel, over-the-knee boots as a biker would be at a cotillion.

She nibbled her lower lip, tasted the lipstick she was chewing off and stopped.

Pam, the gift shop manager at the Diamond Dust, waved from a doorway to the right of the bar. Yvonne glanced behind her before realizing Pam was waving at her. She lifted a hand in return, and then, feeling the weight of more than a few blatantly curious stares on her, she wound her way around the small, square tables toward her coworker.

"Hey," Pam said over the music. "Good to see you."

"Thank you." And how pathetic was it that out of the fifty or so people in the room—some dancing, most just sitting or standing as they chatted—Pam was probably the only one who was happy Yvonne was there?

What was even more pathetic was how much it bothered her.

The song changed. Still country, but with decidedly less twang. "Oh, I love this one," Pam said as she motioned Kathleen and Janice, two women who worked with her at the store, onto the dance floor. "Want to join us?"

Yvonne gaped. Join them? On the dance floor? Trying to move to the heavy, driving beat of the song? She'd make a complete fool of herself. "No, but thank you so much for asking. I think I'll just go find the guest of honor."

Already on her way to the dance floor, Pam waved.

Yvonne glanced around the room. Thankfully, Connie, with her spiky hair and long, willowy body, was easy to spot. She sat at the end of another bar, all the way across the room. Pulling her shoulders back, Yvonne kept her head held high as she made her way toward her nemesis.

Several men, including Mark Michaels, stopped what they were doing to watch her. Yvonne smiled and kept going, as if her face wasn't burning from them all checking her out. By the time she reached Connie, all she wanted was to go home.

"Happy birthday," she said to her.

Connie raised her eyebrows. Matt stood to her right, and seated to her left was a very unhappy looking, very sexy and slightly rumpled Aidan. Yvonne glanced at him only to jerk her gaze away when she met his eyes. He looked…hard. Angry.

They hadn't spoken more than a few times since he'd taken her for that tour of the vineyards. Which was fine with Yvonne. Being with him that way, seeing him relaxed, smiling, made it too easy to forget why she'd left him in the first place.

"I didn't think you'd show," Connie said.

Yvonne's face heated. "I appreciated your gracious invitation so much, how could I resist?"

Actually, it wasn't Connie's invitation, which went something like, "Matt's throwing me a birthday party at the Empire tonight. You should come." It was the fact that she'd bothered to include Yvonne at all. Even if she hadn't called her about the party until late this afternoon.

"You invited her?" Aidan asked.

Both women ignored him. "Relax," Connie said with one of her sharp grins. "I'm glad you came. I just wasn't sure you would." And she sent a sidelong look in Aidan's direction.

Yvonne couldn't bring herself to look at him, though she could feel the weight of his gaze on her. "Yes, well, I do like to keep people guessing." She smoothed her hair behind her ear. Remembered the present in her purse. "And I…well, I got you a little something," she said, pulling out the small, brightly wrapped box. "Happy birthday."

"You already said that," Connie noted, taking it.

Yvonne blinked. So she had. "Do you want that present or not?"

Connie's grin was razor sharp, but not without humor. "I'm not sure. I'll let you know after I open it."

Yvonne had to force herself not to fidget while Connie tore off the wrapping. She shouldn't have gotten a gift. It wasn't as if they were close. Or even friendly. Although after their argument earlier in the week, Connie hadn't been as overtly hostile. Still, that didn't mean she deserved a gift....

"Wow. These are great," Connie said, holding up the silver, filigree drop earrings. "You didn't have to get me anything—but I'm glad you did. Thanks."

Relieved, Yvonne smiled. "You're—"

"J.C.," she continued, calling someone behind Yvonne's shoulders as she held up the jeweler's box. "Look what I got."

J.C. Jane Cleo, Brady's new wife.

"Pretty," said the very pregnant brunette with a round, open face and incredibly curly hair. She leaned forward to get a better look at the earrings. "You must be Yvonne," she said with a warm grin. "And these must be from you."

"Yes." Wincing at how defensive that one word sounded, she added, "I found them at a little store on Main Street."

"Bijou?"

She nodded. "It's a lovely shop." And not something she'd expected in Jewell.

Dear Lord, she really was a snob.

"Brenda—that's Brenda Howard, the owner—only sells unique pieces. She's been pretty successful so far, too." J.C. rubbed her stomach and Yvonne had the strongest urge to touch it herself. What did it feel like? Flabby? Hard? What was it like to have a living being growing inside you?

A middle-aged woman diverted J.C.'s attention. Feeling awkward and unsure, Yvonne searched for an empty seat. A bar stool or chair…a nice dark corner where she could hide. Someplace she could have one drink before politely making her excuses.

She shifted, switched her purse to her other hand. "Well, I'll just…leave you all to enjoy your evening."

"No need to rush off," Connie said as the song changed to something slow and seductive. "You can have my seat." She slid to her feet. "Matt's going to dance with me."

Matt's mouth quirked into a lopsided grin. "That so? I must be a lucky man."

"True," Connie said, taking his hand and tugging him toward the dance floor. "So very true."

Yvonne watched them as they reached the small dance floor. Matt pulled Connie into his arms and they swayed to the music, her head on his shoulder, his hands pressed against the small of her back.

"They look good together," Yvonne murmured, surprised by that. Connie was so cynical and abrasive, while Matt was all flash and charm.

"She deserves better," Aidan said, but without heat. "But, yeah, they're both happy. For now. You going to sit down?"

"Excuse me?"

"You look like you're about to jump out of your skin. Sit down. Have a drink."

So much for acting as if she was relaxed and happy to be here. "I have no idea what you're talking about," she said stiffly, sitting on the stool Connie had vacated. "I'll have a glass of the house white," she told the bartender.

"No, she won't," Aidan said. "She'll have the pinot gris."

She set her purse on her lap, her fingers tense. "I'm capable of ordering for myself," she said when the bartender left to fill her order. Make that Aidan's order.

"I realize that. But the Empire isn't known for its wine selection, and the house white isn't worth drinking." He held her gaze. "Trust me."

She nodded slowly, her breath backed up in her lungs. When the bartender set her wine down, she opened her purse and pulled out her wallet.

"I've got it," Aidan said.

"Oh, that's not necess—"

"I insist," he said quietly.

"Thank you," she gushed. "That's sweet of you."

"Don't."

She forced a smile and took a sip of her wine. "Don't what?"

"Don't pull that Southern belle act on me. If you're

offended or pissed because I want to buy your drink, say so. Don't pretend. Not with me."

She took another sip, this one longer. "You were right," she said, changing the subject. "This wine is lovely. Thank you for suggesting it."

He studied her intently. She lowered her eyes.

"Glad you like it," he finally said.

She traced her fingertip around the rim of her glass. "Is the selection here the reason you're not drinking wine?" she asked, referring to the tumbler of what looked like Scotch in front of him.

"No."

That was it. No explanation, no reason for his drink choice or why he sat in this corner by himself when he was in a room surrounded by his family, friends and coworkers.

She swiveled in her seat to look at him. "Is…are you all right?"

He cupped both hands around his glass. "I'm fine."

But he wasn't. She could see it. She laid her hand on his wrist. His skin was warm; the muscles under her fingers flexed. "Are you sure?"

For a moment she thought he was going to answer her. His gaze went from her hands against his skin, up to her eyes. And in them she saw something that told her he was suffering. It wasn't anger, or at least not just anger, but pain. Fear. And underneath it all, desire. Hunger. Need.

For her.

She slid her hand away.

His mouth curled at her cowardice. "I'm fine," he repeated.

"Good. That's…good." She reached for her wine, but bumped the glass.

"Easy," Aidan murmured, catching it before it tipped over.

"I'm nervous," she blurted, soaking up the drops of spilled wine with a paper napkin.

"You don't say?" His tone was low and amused, his eyes watchful. "And why is that?"

Because he was looking at her differently. Because he was acting strangely. He was making her feel a mixture of anticipation and want and heat that she'd never felt before. Not even when they'd been together.

"I…I know it sounds silly, but I feel like everyone's staring at me," she said, unwilling to confess the rest.

"Everyone *is* staring at you."

"Wonderful. So glad to know I'm not suffering from paranoia."

He sipped his drink. "You command attention, whether you want it or not. And they stare at you because you're beautiful. Sometimes I think you're the most beautiful thing this town has ever seen."

Her mouth went dry. He sounded sincere. Unfortunately, he didn't sound happy about her.

She took another drink. "I don't see Marlene," she said casually. "Is she meeting you here?"

"No."

Yvonne tapped her toe against the rung of the bar stool in agitation. You'd think the man didn't know how to give any other answer to a simple question. "Is she working? Or does Connie dislike her as much as she does me."

"Connie likes her just fine." Of course she did. "Marlene and I aren't seeing each other anymore."

Yvonne's heart seemed to stop beating. In any other situation, she'd be worried that she was experiencing some sort of medical emergency, but now all she cared about was hearing what Aidan had to say. "I'm so sorry to hear that," she said, the lie sounding smooth and sincere, she almost believed it herself. "You two seemed... well suited."

"We were. But it wasn't fair for me to keep seeing her." He lifted his glass but didn't drink. "When I kept thinking about you."

Yvonne had to grab a hold of the bar to keep from falling off the stool. Her pulse pounded in her ears.

"Hi, Yvonne," Mark Michaels said, walking over from his spot at the front of the bar. His gaze took her in. "You look great.... Hey, Aidan."

She pasted on a smile. "Thank you. Enjoying your evening?"

He leaned an elbow on the bar and grinned. "I'd enjoy it a lot more if you'd dance with me."

Another fast song started. "I'm afraid I'm not a very good dancer."

"Now, I don't believe that for a minute," Mark said lightly.

He was right. She knew how to dance. Years of ballet had taught her grace and balance, and her mother had insisted she take dancing lessons as a preteen to master the waltz and other formal dances she'd performed countless times at country club events. But to get out on a dance floor and move to the music without a plan or guidelines on where to step, how to sway? She couldn't.

Had never let herself.

"Come on," he cajoled. "If it'll make you feel better, I can teach you a few steps. It'll be fun."

Fun.

Why don't you just let loose a little? Maybe you'll even have fun.

She had enjoyed herself with Aidan, had even enjoyed riding in that souped up golf cart during their tour. But he'd been right. She didn't often do something just for the sheer pleasure it would give her in return. Why shouldn't she do so now? After all, Mark was a perfectly nice, handsome man. A man who was obviously interested in her. A man who seemed happy with the persona she presented, who wouldn't try to dig deeper. He was safe.

Unlike the man next to her.

"Thank you," she said, getting to her feet. "I'd love to dance."

Except she didn't know what to do with her bag. A problem Mark solved by plucking it from her and setting it on the bar. "Aidan won't mind watching your purse, will you?"

Before Aidan could confirm or deny that statement, Mark placed his hand on the small of her back and led her to the dance floor.

"IF YOU KILL HIM," Connie said when she came back, a few minutes after Yvonne had vacated the seat, "we won't have anyone to finish renovating the carriage house."

Aidan flicked an irritated glance at her, then went back to watching Yvonne. And Mark. "Go enjoy your party."

Instead of listening—why couldn't everyone just do what he wanted?—she sat down. "How can I enjoy it when I'm worried I'll have to stop you from committing murder? If looks could kill, poor Mark would be six feet under right now."

He sipped his Jack Daniels. *Poor Mark my ass.* His blood boiled as he watched the contractor twirl Yvonne, then stop her momentum with a hand to her waist. A hand that stayed there despite the song's upbeat tempo. The son of a bitch.

"Wow," Connie said after ordering another soda, "she is horrible. And here I thought the great Yvonne Delisle could do no wrong. But the way she's moving out there?" She shook her head sadly. "That is nothing *but* wrong."

Aidan grunted. She was right. Yvonne was out of

her element. Her movements were jerky and stiff; the smile she gave Mark—the son of a bitch—was strained. She was nervous and unsure of herself and way too self-conscious to just let go and enjoy the moment.

Good. He didn't want her enjoying any moments. Not with Mark. Not with any other man but him.

Aidan downed the rest of his drink, savoring the burn as it hit his throat. He ordered another one.

Connie watched him as she sipped her soda through a straw.

"If you have something to say," he growled, "just say it."

"Did I misjudge her?"

That was the last thing he expected out of his smart-ass friend. "What?"

"Yvonne. Was I too judgmental about her when you two were together?"

"Why worry about it now?"

"I don't know. I just…I guess maybe I'm wondering if she's really as cold and unfeeling as I always thought she was."

"She is," he said, staring at his new drink. "Everything else is just an act."

"I'm not so sure.…"

"Don't tell me you're starting to like her."

"I think she might actually be growing on me," Connie admitted, sounding shocked by the realization. "Sort of like mold. One day you look, and the loaf of bread that was fine yesterday now has green spots. You can't control it."

No, you couldn't control mold. But he sure as hell could control his tumultuous feelings about his ex-wife.

The song ended and another one started. A slow one, perfect for holding a woman close, swaying with her to the melodic beat. Aidan was on his feet before he even realized it.

"Don't cause a scene," Connie warned him softly as he brushed past her.

He didn't plan on causing a scene. But he'd be damned if he'd sit by and watch his wife in the arms of another man.

"Mind if I have this dance?" he asked, reaching them just as Mark held out his arms for her to step into his embrace.

Mark met his eyes, and what he saw must've been enough to convince him not to argue. "Sure. Thanks for the dance, Yvonne. I'll see you both at work Monday."

Aidan stood next to Yvonne as they watched Mark weave his way through the swaying couples on the floor. "Well," she said in that haughty tone he both hated and loved, "that was incredibly rude."

She turned to leave, but he grabbed her hand. "Dance with me." When she tried to pull free, he held firm and closed the distance between them so he could speak directly into her ear. "Please," he added quietly.

At her acquiescence, he tugged her into his arms. He kept his hands at her waist and started moving to the music. She was stiff, her hands on his shoulders, her gaze somewhere over his left ear.

"You know I'm not very good at this," she said, her body leaning away from his, her feet shuffling back and forth.

"You're doing fine. Just relax." He slowly pulled her closer until their thighs brushed. Her eyes widened. "You're thinking too much," he said, settling his hands at the small of her back, his fingers brushing the top of her ass. "Stop worrying about what you look like, what people think of you. Just listen to the music."

She nodded, her expression serious, as if he was going to quiz her on this later. But she inhaled deeply, and when she exhaled, her shoulders relaxed a bit and her fingers stopped digging into his skin.

"Come a little closer," he said softly.

She hesitated. He continued moving, swaying to the hypnotic beat, and finally, thankfully, she stepped closer. Her hips bumped his, her breasts pressed lightly against his chest. His body tightened painfully.

He turned his head, inhaled the sweet scent of her hair before breathing into her ear, "Now hold on to me."

Slowly, so slowly it took all he had not to yank her to him while he waited, she slid her hands around the back of his neck. Her fingers were cool against his heated skin, her nails lightly scraping his scalp as she combed them through his hair.

She didn't put her head on his shoulder, but kept her eyes on his as they danced. He led her through the motions with his thighs, his hands, his hips. For every move he made, she matched him, her body lithe and graceful.

Tension seemed to surround them, thickening the air. It didn't matter that they were on a dance floor with a dozen other couples, that his brothers and coworkers were all there, witnessing his weakness for this woman. All that mattered was keeping Yvonne in his arms.

Holding her, feeling her lush curves pressed against him, it was so easy to forget everything else. His mother's diagnosis, the guilt of keeping it from his brothers. He could let go of the pain and anger of the past. The feelings of betrayal. The sense of loss that always accompanied his memories.

But this moment couldn't last. Already the song was winding down. In a matter of seconds he'd have to return to the real world. A world where his mother was sick and the woman in his arms was no longer his. Hadn't been his for a long time.

The song ended, replaced by a faster-paced one. People moved around them, sent them curious glances. Aidan knew he looked like an idiot, standing in the middle of the dance floor with his ex-wife—the woman who'd walked out on him—in his arms. But he wasn't ready to let her go.

She licked her lips, the nervous gesture going straight to his groin. "Aidan—"

He shook his head. Then stepped back so that her

hands fell from his neck, brushing his chest as she lowered her arms.

"Thanks for the dance," he said, itching to pull her close again. He walked away, not making eye contact with anyone as he left the room, crossed through the main bar and out into the cold darkness.

CHAPTER THIRTEEN

WELL OVER AN hour later, Yvonne pulled up in front of the cottage. After Aidan had left her standing on the dance floor like an idiot, she'd gone back to the bar and finished her wine. Chatted with J.C. about the possibility of her providing gourmet chocolates for Diamond Dust weddings. Traded barbs with Connie—except tonight the barbs were good-natured.

She'd done what she did best. She'd put on a show. Appearances, after all, were everything. They kept her safe from people looking too closely.

She doubted anyone even realized anything out of the ordinary had happened. That she'd had a life-altering experience, one that had made her insides feel as twisted as a rope, her emotions a jumbled mess.

Careful not to turn an ankle in her high heels, she crossed the gravel driveway as quickly as possible, the glow of the porch light doing little to dispel the darkness. That was just one of many things she hadn't liked about living in Jewell when she and Aidan had been married. How dark it got at night. She'd missed the glow of the city. The sounds of traffic. How easy it was for her to get lost in a crowd. To be anonymous.

And if no one knew her, she didn't have to worry about who they expected her to be.

Something rustled in the bushes to her right. Her heart raced, but she didn't bolt for the door. She refused to give in to her fears of the unknown. Once a night was enough for that.

Because that's exactly what she'd done at the bar. She'd let her fear of the way Aidan made her feel, of how much he made her *want,* control her. Had been so afraid that she hadn't tried to stop him from leaving her alone on that dance floor.

He wanted her back in his bed.

It wasn't fair for me to keep seeing her. When I kept thinking about you.

Despite everything that'd happened between them, he still wanted her. A scary, scary thought. But also thrilling. And way too tempting.

At the door, she dug her keys from her purse and unlocked the door. A shadow to her left moved. She clenched the keys, ready to defend herself. And then the shape emerged from the darkness.

"Aidan," she breathed. "You scared the life out of me." Squinting, she searched the driveway. "How'd you get here?" Surely she hadn't been so preoccupied that she'd missed seeing his parked car.

"I walked."

"From our…from your house?"

His eyes flashed. "I stopped by my mom's to check

on her, but when I went out to drive home I started walking, and ended up here."

"Why?"

His gaze dropped to her mouth.

Her heart hammered against her ribs. Oh, God. Yes, she knew exactly why he was here. They'd been married, had had sex hundreds of times. But she'd never before felt this anticipation, this mix of longing and pure need. Had never had him look at her with such all-consuming hunger and heat. As if he wanted her beyond hope, beyond reason.

Aidan had always desired her, had always expected her to give him everything she wanted to keep to herself—her thoughts and feelings. The more he'd pushed, the deeper she'd gone inside herself, too afraid to fully open up to the man who'd claimed to love her. The man she'd vowed to love for the rest of her life. And now he stood in front of her wanting her to share her body with him.

He reached out and traced a fingertip from her temple to her jawline. "Are you going to invite me in?"

Nerves made it impossible to speak. His hair was messed, as if he'd run his hands through it repeatedly. His jacket was open. He smelled of fresh air and the musky scent that was unique to him. He was the only man she'd ever loved, the only man she'd ever wanted to love her. But they'd made so many mistakes.

"I don't think—"

"I want you, Yvonne."

She could see that as clearly as she saw the twitching of his jaw. He'd walked away from her on the dance floor but he was here now, risking his pride. He didn't love her anymore. She wasn't sure he ever really had. He didn't need her. But he wanted her.

She wanted him, too.

"Come inside," she whispered, reaching behind her to open the door. Holding his gaze, she stepped backward over the threshold.

She had no idea what to do, if she should go to him or let him come to her. Out of her element once again. So she didn't do anything, just waited inside the doorway.

He followed her in, his mouth a hard line. Her head grew light and she realized she was holding her breath. She exhaled softly. Stopping in front of her, he placed his hands on her hips and slowly dragged her toward him, giving her time. A chance to change her mind.

She laid her hands on his chest. Felt the frantic beat of his heart, the way his fingers tightened on her hips. He wasn't as steady or in control as she'd thought. Warmth pooled in her stomach.

His narrowed gaze skimmed her face. Sliding an arm around her, he pulled her flush against him. She locked her knees so they wouldn't buckle, curled her fingers into the hard planes of his chest. Each breath she took caused her breasts to brush against him, tugged the silk of her shirt tighter. Her nipples beaded. Her skin heated.

He gently outlined her mouth with his fingertip. Lightly rubbed the indentation above her upper lip. He pulled his hand away, scowled at the faint red mark left by her lipstick. He moved his free hand to the nape of her neck, held her head still while he rubbed the thumb of his other hand across her mouth, wiping off her lipstick.

And then he crushed his mouth down on hers as he walked her farther into the tiny entryway. He kicked the door shut behind them, the sound reverberating through the house, through her veins. His kiss was wild. Rough. And a touch mean.

She wanted to kiss him back just as hungrily, to devour him, but she'd never felt this level of desire before. When they were together before, their lovemaking had been more reserved. Civilized. Nothing this desperate, this edgy. Panic suffused her. Had her squirming against him. When he didn't so much as loosen his hold, she reached up and tugged his hair. Hard.

He lifted his head. His eyes glittered; his breathing was choppy. She felt the tension of his restraint, what it cost him to hold back.

His eyes on hers, he slid his hand from her hair the top of her breast, his palm over her racing heart. She searched his eyes, saw the power she had over him, power that was both humbling and exhilarating.

"Be with me," he said, his voice guttural. "Just for one night, let it be you and me and nothing else."

Instead of answering, she tightened her hold on his hair and pulled his mouth back to hers.

He groaned and deepened the kiss as he gently squeezed her breast. She arched and pushed herself into his hand. Still kissing her, he walked her backward. Her shoulders hit the wall with a soft thud, but he kept moving closer, trapping her between the heat of his solid body and the cold drywall. He bit kisses along her neck as he slid his thigh between her legs. It was all she could do not to rub against him in an effort to ease the ache there.

He nibbled her earlobe and she gasped. Lifting his head, he tugged her shirt out of her jeans. She jerked at the feel of his work-roughened palm against the sensitive skin of her stomach. He trailed his hands across her rib cage, shoved her shirt and bra up until they were bunched under her armpits. Then he lifted her arms, trapping them overhead with one large hand bracketed around her wrists, then took a tight nipple into his mouth and sucked.

She bucked against him, but he didn't loosen his hold. Her breath shuddered in and out. He lightly scraped his teeth over the tip of her breast and she went wild. Breaking his hold, she clawed at his back, yanking his shirt over his head so she could smooth her palms over the solid planes of his chest, the muscles bunching at his shoulders.

She pushed against him so that they reversed positions and he was against the wall. He kissed her and turned them again. And again. Until they were in the hallway outside the bedroom door.

He pressed her hard into the wall, nudged her head back with one hand as he kissed her jaw, the line of her throat. His free hand slid down her stomach to the waistband of her jeans. Her hips lifted as he undid the button and zipper.

"The bed…"

But she trailed off when he shook his head, his eyes hot with want. Dropping to his knees in front of her, he unzipped her boots, the sound loud in the stillness. He slid first one boot, then the other off, tossing them aside before reaching up and dragging her jeans and panties down her legs. His movements were so slow, so deliberate she wanted to yell at him to hurry up. Or grab her pants and cover herself again. She stood pressed against the wall, her fingers curled into her palms, her head tipped back as she stared at the white ceiling.

He pulled her clothes to her ankles, then skimmed one finger up her leg, along her inner thigh. Her pelvis contracted. "You're so beautiful." He traced that finger along the crease where her thigh and hip bone connected, then lightly over her tight curls. She bit her lip. "I still dream about you."

He massaged her thighs, his strong hands turning her muscles to jelly. She moaned, the low, rasping sound seeming to come from someone else. But, oh, she dreamed of him, too. Missed him too much.

"Let me in, Yvonne." He kissed the juncture of her thighs and she stiffened. But he held her firmly, his fingers tight on her rear, his thumbs pressing her hip bones. "Just this once, let me in."

Her breath lodged in her chest. She couldn't. She was too exposed, her shirt bunched up and her jeans at her ankles, her body open for him to see. If she wasn't careful, he'd see inside her heart.

But he was rubbing circles on her hips, her abdomen. His breath was hot on her, his naked chest brushing against her legs. And when he leaned forward and licked her, she couldn't fight it any longer. She groaned and let her thighs relax.

It didn't matter that she was writhing under his hands and mouth, with no sense of who she was, of what she should be doing, how she should be acting. Her hips moved against him as she sought relief from the building pressure. Guttural sounds rose from her throat, mixed with her raspy breathing. And when she glanced down, saw him on his knees in front of her, her manicured nails in his hair as she held his head to the most intimate part of her, that pressure burst.

She cried out, her fingers tightening, digging into his scalp as her orgasm rocked her. Shock wave after shock wave convulsed her, again and again.

Gasping for breath, her body shaking, she felt Aidan lift her foot. She could barely move as he took her jeans off. He lurched to his feet, his movements frantic as he took a condom out of his pocket, then pushed his pants down, freeing his erection. She reached out to touch him, wanting to hold that hardness, that heat, in her hand. But he was already sheathing himself.

"Hold on to me," he commanded, the same words he'd said when they'd been dancing.

She wound her arms around his neck, watched his face as he gripped her thighs and slid inside her.

AIDAN GROUND HIS TEETH, fought against the urge to pound into Yvonne. Until he'd rid himself of this incessant need for her.

But when he'd entered her, she'd rolled her eyes back as if it had been the best thing she'd ever felt.

He could relate.

He shifted, lifting her higher in his arms, going deeper inside her. She gasped and then moaned as he bent his head and kissed her. Her mouth was hot and wet under his, her tongue touching his. She smelled of her perfume and sex. He couldn't get enough of her.

And what would that mean when it was time for her to walk away again?

He leaned back and waited until she blinked up at him, until her eyes focused on his. Her hair was damp with sweat, her eye makeup smudged, her lipstick smeared.

She'd never been more beautiful to him.

"Hold on," he repeated, and this time she gripped his shoulders, her nails digging into his skin, and locked her ankles around his waist.

To his surprise, she leaned forward and kissed him, a soft, sweet kiss that warmed his insides.

Except, that wasn't he wanted. He deepened the kiss, turned carnal as he moved inside her.

This time, when she went over that edge, she took him with her.

YVONNE GASPED FOR AIR, her heart pounding. Aidan's face was pressed against her neck, his chest rising and falling heavily against her. Her body was slick with sweat. She was pleasantly sore. Completely satiated.

And Aidan was still inside her.

Oh, God. What had she done?

She wriggled and he straightened, slowly lowering her legs until her feet touched the floor. Her entire body trembled with the aftereffects of her second orgasm, with the effort it took to remain upright. She picked up her clothes and took a shaky step forward. Then another. Satisfied she wasn't about to slide into a boneless heap at his feet, she bolted across the hall into the bathroom and firmly shut the door behind her.

Yanking up her panties, she caught sight of her reflection in the mirror and winced. She wriggled back into her jeans, then adjusted her bra and shirt, her cheeks heating at how…wanton she looked. How she'd acted.

She ran cold water over a cloth, then pressed it to her neck, her face. They'd made love in the hall, against the wall. It had been frantic and basic and rushed. Unlike anything she'd ever experienced before. It had been wonderful.

But it hadn't been making love. Frowning at herself, she lowered the cloth. And, dear God, she'd liked it. She shouldn't have. It wasn't proper. He'd stripped her of more than just her clothes, he'd stripped her of her inhibitions. Of her barriers.

She squeezed the cloth until her hand hurt. She needed those barriers. So she went to work putting them back in place.

Ten minutes later, when she opened the door, her clothes were straight, her hair brushed and her makeup reapplied. She stepped out into the hall, her heart in her throat. But Aidan wasn't there. Actually, there was no sign anything had happened between them at all. Certainly nothing that pointed out how stupid she'd been to let him make her lose control like that.

"I see you've put your mask back on."

She gasped and turned toward the sound of that sardonic voice, to find Aidan standing in the kitchen by the sink. "I...I thought you'd left."

Had hoped if she took long enough to gather her thoughts, he would leave.

"No such luck." His shirt was wrinkled, hanging loose from his jeans. His hair stuck up at odd angles and she blushed, remembering exactly what he'd been doing when she'd had her hands in his hair. How much she'd enjoyed it.

And yet, though he was a far cry from looking put

together, he was still obviously in control. She needed to take a lesson from him.

She smiled. "I'm sorry I took so long. Can I get you something? A glass of wine or—"

"Knock it off," he growled.

Flustered, she clasped her hands together in front of her waist. "I'm sorry, I don't understand."

"Knock off the act, the whole charade you've got going here with the clothes and the makeup and the polite veneer." He shook his head, disgusted. Disappointed. "Hell, maybe that's all there is to you. Maybe there's nothing real about you at all."

She locked her shaking knees. "I'm very real."

"You're not," he said quietly, his eyes narrowed as he studied her. "You're all appearance."

"I don't think having pride in one's appearance is a crime."

"You're good at that," he murmured almost thoughtfully as he moved toward her. "Excellent at saying what you think people want to hear. At keeping people at a distance. I thought you were just cold. Above everyone and everything. But now I can't help but wonder if you're not hiding behind all that. Tell me, what are you afraid of?"

His words cut deep. She glanced down at herself, surprised they hadn't drawn blood.

What was she afraid of? She was afraid of this. Of letting someone get close enough to hurt her.

"I'm not hiding. I've just learned that people only

see what they want to see. Women see me as a snob. A conceited rich girl. A threat. Men often convince themselves I'm an ice princess—and they're the only one who can turn me on, who can thaw me out. Or they assume I'm an angel with my fussy clothes and makeup. That I'll be sweet and malleable, easy for them to shape into whatever they're looking for." She sneered. "It seems I'm some sort of fantasy."

"I'm not sure who you're giving less credit," he said. "Any man who might be interested in you, or yourself."

"I'm being honest. People don't want me because of who I am," she said, proud of how strong her voice was, how steadily she met Aidan's eyes. "In school, the other kids only wanted to be friends with me because of my last name. As I got older and realized it, I learned how to protect myself."

His nostrils flared. "By playing some part? Putting on an act?"

"By giving people what they want." Setting her hands on her hips, she flipped her hair back. "Wasn't that why you wanted me? Why you pursued me? You wanted this—" She held out her arms. "The package. And that's exactly what you got, but when we moved to Jewell, suddenly it wasn't enough."

"I was attracted to your looks, yes," he admitted tightly, his mouth barely moving, "but that wasn't why I asked you to marry me. I fell in love with you. Despite how standoffish and aloof you were, despite how you shut me out, I loved you."

Just when she thought he couldn't possibly hurt her any more than he already had, he proved her wrong. But underneath that hurt, her anger simmered.

"How magnanimous of you, marrying me despite my many flaws. Tell me, Aidan," she demanded, stalking toward him, her hands fisted, "was that why you were constantly trying to get me to act a certain way? Why you wanted so badly to change me?"

He flinched as if she'd slapped him. "I didn't want to change you. I tried to get you to open up to me, to be real with me."

"That is such…such…bullshit." His eyebrows shot upward, whether at her cursing or because she was now yelling, she wasn't sure. All she knew was that her heart was aching. She began to pace. "You're just like my parents, just like my ex-fiancé. You all claim to love me when I'm what you want. When I'm who you want me to be. The dutiful daughter. The beautiful, malleable fiancée. You didn't want me to open up to you. You wanted me to be someone else. Connie. Or your mother. Someone who enjoyed schlepping around outside or spending hours in the kitchen. Who laughed at those stupid movies you watched. Who made friends easily and was interested in small town gossip."

"Is that what you really thought? That I wanted you to be someone else?" he asked after a moment of stunned silence. He shoved an unsteady hand through his hair. "My God, is that why you left me?"

There's one question you've never asked. Why I left.

Well, he was asking it now, his brows lowered, his mouth a grim line, his gaze bewildered as if he really was clueless.

"I was never enough. I wasn't comfortable with public displays of affection. I didn't cook or bake. I hated my job at the hospital, couldn't relate to my co-workers." Her stomach cramped and she hugged her arms around herself. "I was too staid. Too uptight. Too guarded with my thoughts and emotions."

And the more he'd pushed her, the more he'd actively tried to break down those barriers, the harder she'd fought him.

She laughed, but felt no humor. "Want to know the really funny part? I fell in love with you, and married you because I thought you loved me, that you accepted me for who I was. Kept trying to convince myself of that until you decided it was time for us to have a baby."

His nostrils flared. "Hold on. I didn't decide anything. I brought up the subject of us starting a family, that was all." The corded muscles of his neck stood out. "If you weren't ready to have children, you could've said something instead of leaving."

"What difference would it have made? You wanted me to be yet someone else—a mother. But how could I take on another role when I wasn't even sure who I was?" Her eyes burned. "I'll never be Connie or your mother or your fantasy version of the perfect wife. I'm just me. That wasn't good enough for you—"

Her voice broke. She swallowed and forced herself to hold his gaze.

"That wasn't good enough for you," she repeated. "But it's finally good enough for me."

CHAPTER FOURTEEN

YVONNE'S CELL PHONE vibrated, the low buzzing too loud in the quiet dining room. Her face heated as all eyes went to her. "Excuse me," she said, setting down her fork so she could reach in her bag on the floor next to her.

She glanced at the screen, saw the familiar number. Manners dictated she send it directly to voice mail. After all, she was at a business function. Sort of. At least, that's how she preferred to think of this weekly Thursday lunch with the Sheppard family.

Purely business.

But this hadn't exactly been a normal lunch. For one thing, J.C. was there. And from Yvonne could tell, her only ties to the winery were Brady and the chocolates she sold in the gift shop. For another, there was an undercurrent of tension. All she knew was that it was uncomfortable as a cheap pair of four-inch stilettos.

"I'm so sorry," she said, smiling in apology as she stood, "but it's my mother. She would never call me during work hours unless it was important." Which was such a blatant lie Yvonne was surprised the good Lord didn't fry her on the spot. "If you all will excuse me?"

She hurried out of the room and into the kitchen. "Mother. Hello. How are you?"

"I'm well, dear, thank you," Elaine said, the heavy tones of the South not softening her cool, cultured voice one bit. "It's you I'm worried about."

Whining, Lily bumped Yvonne's leg. She made a shooing motion but the dog just bumped her again, looking up at her with sad eyes. "Worried? About me?"

"Of course. But then, I suppose that's what parents do when they don't hear from their children for weeks at a time."

The worst part? She knew her mother really did worry about her and loved her—in her own way. Just as she knew Elaine wasn't above using that worry or that love to try to control her only child.

Yvonne paced the length of the bar, Lily on her heels. "I'm so sorry I haven't called. I've just been swamped with work." Diane had laid out the makings for sandwiches on the island—three different breads, various meats and cheeses, lettuce, tomato slices and several condiments. There were also chips, pretzels and a large pan of frosted brownies. "Actually, I'm due in a meeting in a few minutes. Can I call you back tonight?"

Elaine sighed. "That won't be necessary. I just wanted to make sure you were all right. And to go over your plans for next month."

"Next month?"

"When you come down to Savannah," Elaine said airily. "Now, I realize Charleston is only a few hours away, but I sincerely hope you plan to spend the night."

In the act of sneaking a piece of sliced ham to Lily—even she couldn't resist a sad dog—Yvonne froze, the hair on her arms standing on end. "Spend the night?"

"Don't repeat everything I say, dear, it's rude."

"Yes, ma'am," she said absently, racking her brain to figure out what in the world this was about.

"As I was saying, your father and I would love for you to stay the night—or the entire weekend. We just don't see enough of you."

"Mother, I'm sorry but I have no idea what you're talking about. Why do you think I'm coming to Savannah next month?"

"Oh, Yvonne, don't tell me you've forgotten," her mother said with an irritated sigh. "You know perfectly well your father and I host our annual fundraiser for the children's wing of the hospital the third Saturday in April. Why, it's been a tradition in the Delisle family since your great-grandfather donated the money to create the wing."

She cut a small square of brownie and popped it into her mouth, chewed and swallowed before saying, "I didn't forget. It just…slipped my mind for a moment, that's all. I…I wouldn't miss it."

"Wonderful. And don't worry about finding an escort. Kenneth said he'd be thrilled to accompany you. Isn't that sweet?"

"Yes," she managed to say, "that's very…kind of him."

Picking up a butter knife from the counter, she mimed jabbing the end of it into her temple. Repeatedly.

Her parents had invited Kenneth—current vice president of business development at Delisle Enterprises—to dinner the last time she'd been home. He'd made it perfectly clear to her that his burning ambition to one day run her father's company was surpassed only by his desire to marry her. Because by attaining his first goal, by tying himself to her, he'd be sure to reach his second goal.

She eyed the brownies. Shrugged, then cut herself another small piece. "Mother, I'm really sorry, but I do have to go." She glanced into the dining room to see Connie saying something to Aidan, her hands flat on the table. Whatever it was darkened Aidan's expression. "I'll call you this weekend. Love you."

She ended the call, then shut off her phone. Her entire life, all she'd ever wanted was for her parents to be proud of her. To love her. And they were—did—on their terms.

Connie's voice rose, followed by Aidan's low reply.

Yvonne wiped a speck of chocolate frosting from her thumb with a paper napkin. "I'd much rather stay out here with you," she told Lily. The dog tipped her head to the side.

It had been five days since Yvonne's honest—and impassioned—speech to Aidan. He hadn't denied he'd tried to mold her into who he'd wanted her to be, he'd simply walked out.

She hadn't cried, she thought now as she dropped more ham on the floor for Lily. She'd been too angry. Too hurt.

She'd let him inside that night, had sex with him because she'd foolishly thought he saw her, the real her. That he wanted to be with the woman she was now.

She'd thought this time would be different.

Instead, she'd had to do her best to treat Aidan politely, professionally, for the past five days. To pretend, as effectively as he did, that that night hadn't happened.

Thankfully, she had her work to keep her busy, to keep her mind off him. The renovations on the carriage house were coming along, and if they didn't run into any problems with the weather or any delays in shipping materials Mark would need, it should be complete by Diane and Al's wedding at the end of next week. Using Aidan's list of contacts, she'd come up with over a dozen preferred vendors they could work with, and the tables and chairs she'd ordered were due to arrive next week.

And there was more to do. She had policies and guidelines to come up with. Had to figure out deposit and rental fees, and discuss with Aidan and his brothers how much of a discount to offer on wine being served at future events. She had to research the legalities of having the caterers provide beer or other alcohol, with the proper license. Noise ordinances for music. Insurance and liability issues.

Not to mention all the work still needed for the senator and Diane's wedding.

Yes, she certainly had enough to keep her busy. And her mind off her ex-husband.

"For now," she murmured to the dog, "I have to get through this meal."

As she walked back into the dining room, Connie shouted at Aidan, "Because I don't want to do it!" She pointed at Yvonne. "Ask her. She'll tell you how uninterested I am in event planning."

Yvonne's step faltered. "Excuse me?"

But neither Aidan nor Connie seemed to hear her. "This whole new venture was your idea," he said.

Connie nodded sharply, her chin jutting. "I know that."

"And now you don't want to do it?"

"No, I don't," she said through gritted teeth. "I'd rather be out in the vineyards where I belong. Look, we both know..." She gestured around the table at their rapt audience. "We all know a big part of the reason I suggested we start hosting events in the first place was so I'd have a position at the Diamond Dust in case Matt went through with the partnership. I just...wanted some sort of guarantee that you'd all keep me around," she admitted softly.

Yvonne's lips parted. And here she'd thought Connie was so confident in her place with the Sheppards. Had envied the other woman's inclusion in their family, how easily they accepted her.

"You've discussed the job details of event planning with Connie," Aidan said and it took a moment for Yvonne to realize he was talking to her. "What do you think? Can she handle it?"

Oh, no. No way was she getting involved in this. It was true she'd spent Tuesday evening at Connie's house, explaining an event manager's responsibilities and yes, Connie had seemed less than interested.

Not her problem, Yvonne assured herself as she retook her seat. "I'm afraid I'm not comfortable giving my opinion," she said.

An opinion he had no right to ask for. This wasn't her company. Wasn't her family. Soon she'd be back in Charleston where she belonged. Back to World Class Weddings and her clients and her lonely apartment.

"This is my fault," Diane said quietly from the head of the table. She looked at Connie. "I'm so sorry. I never meant to hurt you. And I certainly never meant to do anything that would make you think you wouldn't have a place here. That you weren't a part of this family."

Yvonne stared at the table and hoped no one could see how much she wished Diane was saying those things to her.

"But you did," Matt said to his mother as he slid his arm around Connie's shoulders. "You didn't care about how your decisions would affect any of us. All you cared about was yourself."

"Shut up," Aidan growled, his hands fisted on the table.

Matt bristled. Let go of Connie so he could turn in his chair and face his eldest brother, his expression hard. "The hell I will. What did the old man always tell us? That our actions have consequences. Well, now she has to deal with those consequences, good or bad."

Aidan rose part way from his seat. "You don't know what you're talking about."

Diane held out a hand. "No, that's all right, Aidan." She inhaled deeply. "You're right, Matt. I have to live with the choices I've made. And I know you're still angry about my forcing you back to the Diamond Dust. I know you...you may never forgive me."

"I didn't say that." Matt tipped his head from side to side, then exhaled heavily. "You told me I needed to forgive Dad in order to move on from the past, and you were right. But just because things worked out for the best—" he stroked a hand over Connie's short hair "—doesn't mean I like how you got me here. You took away my choices."

"I did. I'm so sorry. I was desperate. And afraid you'd never come back." Diane pressed her trembling lips together and reached over for her fiancé's hand, clutching it so hard, her knuckles turned white. "I...I have to tell you something." She swallowed. "I'm just not sure I can."

"You can," Aidan said quietly, encouragingly.

Yvonne's stomach clenched. The back of her neck turned cold with apprehension and she pushed her chair back to stand. "Maybe I should leave."

She didn't want to be a part of what was obviously a personal conversation.

"No," Diane said. "Please. This involves you, too, and I'd…I'd really like you to stay."

Yvonne slowly nodded, saw the same fear and nervousness she was feeling on the faces of the people gathered at the table.

Diane sipped her water, her hand unsteady. "I did everything in my power to make sure things turned out how I wanted them to. I wanted my sons to run the winery together so I threatened to sell the Diamond Dust if they didn't all agree." She smiled sadly at Yvonne. "I wanted you and Aidan back together, so I hired you to plan my wedding, to work for us."

Yvonne twisted her napkin in her fingers. She couldn't even glance at Aidan.

"It didn't matter what any of you thought, what plans or dreams you had," Diane continued. "I convinced myself I was doing it for you. That all I wanted was your happiness. And while I do want you to be happy—I want that more than anything—the truth is, I was selfish." She inhaled deeply. "And I'm sorry."

"Okay," Matt said, "now you're freaking me out. Who are you and what have you done with our real mother?"

"Not funny," Aidan snapped.

Diane cleared her throat. "There's no easy way to say this…"

"Just tell us," Brady said in his low voice. J.C. laid her hand on his forearm on top of the table.

Diane nodded. "I have breast cancer."

HEARING HIS MOTHER announce her illness for the second time didn't make it any easier for Aidan to accept. Or to bear. He wanted to punch something.

Everyone except Al was visibly shocked. J.C. brought her hand to her mouth, while Connie shook her head slowly, as if to deny his mother's words. To his right, Yvonne sat back in her seat, but he couldn't look at her fully. Couldn't take the chance he'd meet her eyes. That she'd see the fear he was trying so hard to hide. To fight.

"How bad?" Brady asked.

"Not as bad as it could be," their mother said. "Worse than any of us, including my doctor, would like, of course. I...I had my first chemotherapy treatment Tuesday. My oncologist wants to try and shrink the size of the tumor before surgery."

She'd started treatment. She was going to fight this. Thank God.

"You've known?" Matt asked as he sat at the edge of his seat, his voice hoarse. "You've started treatments and you're just telling us now?"

"I wanted to wait until I was sure..." She met his eyes, then Brady's, then Aidan's. "Until I'd decided whether or not to receive treatment."

The stunned silence was broken when Connie started to cry softly.

"After witnessing how your father... I'm not sure I'm strong enough to fight this," Diane explained.

Aidan's clenched his fists on his thighs. Damn it. He should be able to fix this.

Yvonne laid her hand over his. Her skin was warm, her touch gentle. And more comforting than she could ever know. He shuddered out a quiet breath and turned his hand over, linked his fingers with hers.

Connie didn't even bother wiping away the tears streaking down her face. "You were just going to give up?"

His mother lowered her eyes. "I considered it. But now I'm willing to fight, for as long as it takes, no matter what. I'm fighting for you. For all of you." She looked at Brady and J.C. "I want to see my grandson born. I want to watch him take his first steps, say his first words. I want more Saturday afternoons baking cookies with Payton and Abby." She blinked rapidly. "But it won't be easy. As we all know, there are no guarantees I'll get through this."

Matt shoved a hand through his hair. "God, don't say that."

"I have to say it. If I'm going through treatments, we all have to be realistic about what's to come. What the outcome might be. And we have to be willing to face that outcome, no matter what." Aidan easily recognized the stubborn tilt of her chin. "I may have been... wrong...to force you all into taking over the winery." She looked to Al, who nodded. "And if any of you want to back out of the agreement we made, I won't hold it against you. I won't sell the Diamond Dust."

Aidan squeezed Yvonne's hand so tightly she flinched. He loosened his grip but couldn't let go. For years he'd put his family—what was best for his father's company—first. And now, suddenly, the weight of responsibility he'd carried for the past eight years disappeared. He could walk away from the Diamond Dust and Jewell with no recriminations. No guilt. He could finish law school. Or maybe he'd discover a new dream, a different future.

For the first time in a very long time, he had a choice.

"I'm still in," Brady said.

"Me, too," Matt added gruffly. "There's nowhere I'd rather be than right here."

All focus shifted to Aidan. He raised his head, saw the concern in Yvonne's eyes. The same question that hung in the air. *What would he do?*

He exhaled, and as he did, something inside him broke free. *He had a choice.*

And he knew exactly what he wanted.

"Looks as if things are staying the way you planned," he told his mother. "The Diamond Dust is our future now."

"AIDAN," YVONNE SAID later that night, unable to keep the surprise from her voice. "What are you doing here?"

She winced. No, that hadn't been the most polite thing to say. But honestly, when a man showed up at a woman's door after ten at night, she had the right to know what he wanted. Especially if that man also happened to be your ex-husband who'd barely spoken to you in days, only to cling to your hand when his mother announced she had cancer.

Aidan didn't seem to mind her rudeness. In the dim glow of the porch light his expression was blank, his eyes unreadable. "Can I come in?"

A chill racked her and she pulled the edges of her robe closed. Oh, that was such a bad idea. The least of which being what had happened the last time he'd shown up here unannounced wanting her to let him in.

"It's late," she hedged. "I was just getting ready for bed."

His gaze slid over her, from her damp hair and her face, down the short, fuzzy robe to her bare legs and brightly polished toes. "I don't mean to disrupt your night. I was hoping we could…talk."

She raised her eyebrows. "Talk? Is that what they're calling it these days?"

To her surprise, a flush stained his cheeks. "I just…I need someone to talk to," he admitted, his raspy voice washing over her. "I need *you,* Yvonne."

She caught her breath and tightened her grip on the robe. No. No, no, no. She couldn't let him in. It was late. He had no right to show up here, not after how things had ended between them the other night.

Besides, she wasn't prepared for company. She'd showered earlier and had spent the past hour researching favors for a November wedding she was planning, while catching up on episodes of *Top Chef.* Her hair was drying in frizzy waves; her face was clean of makeup. And all she wore under her favorite, fuzzy robe was a long-sleeved silk caftan that barely reached midthigh.

She was tired. Her emotional barriers were down.

But he needed her. Not some nebulous idea of who he thought she should be. Her.

Stepping back, she opened the door farther. "I'll make coffee."

She padded down the hall, her heart racing. She wanted to run into the bathroom, comb her hair, throw on some foundation—or at the very least mascara and blush. Put on something less revealing. She filled the coffeepot and heard him come into the kitchen, the scrape of the chair against the floor as he sat down. Still, she kept her back to him as she counted out scoops, started the machine.

Once coffee began to drip into the pot, the aroma filling the air, she pulled two cups and saucers from an upper cabinet, took the creamer from the fridge and placed them both on the table along with spoons. She opened the bag of sugar cookies she'd picked up during her last shopping trip, and arranged some on a plate, setting them in front of Aidan before sitting across from him.

He looked so lost. Her heart broke for him. "I'm sorry about your mom," she said.

"She'll beat it."

But he didn't sound convinced. Leaning forward, Yvonne grasped his hand. "She will. She's an incredibly strong woman."

"My dad was strong, too," he said, so quietly she had to strain to hear. "The strongest man I knew. Do you know he never got sick? Always bragged about how he didn't catch so much as a cold, and then one day he complained to Mom of stomach pain. He thought it was food poisoning, then some sort of stomach bug. He didn't even see a doctor until the pain spread to his back." Aidan stroked the back of Yvonne's hand with his thumb, gazing down. "Six months later, he was gone."

Her throat closed. "I remember. I know how hard it was for you, for all of you."

"My dad was a good man. Not perfect by any stretch of the imagination. But even though he made mistakes, he stayed true to who he was without apologizing for it. All my life I've been told how I'm just like him. For so long, I thought that meant I didn't have to apologize for anything, especially not for who I am. But now..." He leaned back and rubbed both hands over his face before meeting her eyes. "I never meant to hurt you, Yvonne."

She hadn't meant to hurt him, either. But she had. She turned a cup on the saucer so the handle was on the right side. "We both made mistakes. I should've told you I was unhappy. Should've explained why I had to leave. Maybe we just...weren't meant to be."

But she was no longer sure she believed that.

He swallowed. "I'm scared."

His words, so soft, so honest, ripped into her. She knew what it cost him to admit that, how hard it was for him to show any weakness.

And he'd come here, opened himself up to her. It wasn't about love. It was more elemental. He needed her. And for tonight, that would be enough for her.

She stood, shut off the coffeepot and circled the table. "Come with me," she said, holding out her hand.

Frowning, he let her pull him to his feet. "Yvonne, what—"

She silenced him with a warm kiss. "I want to make love to you. Let me," she whispered against his mouth. "Let me comfort you. Let me love you."

His fingers tightened on her hand. He searched her eyes. "Are you sure?"

In answer, she tugged him down the hallway to her bedroom. Crossed to the bedside table and turned on the lamp before nudging him down onto the bed. He reached for her but she stepped back.

You're hiding.

He'd been right. She had hid from him. Was still hiding. But not anymore.

With her eyes on his, she undid the tie at her waist, let the robe slide off her arms to pool on the floor at her feet. His breathing quickened in the silence of the room, but he kept his hands clasped loosely between his knees, his gaze hot. Intent.

She stepped between his legs and he straightened.

The silk of her caftan rubbed softly against her thighs. Against her breasts. Her nipples hardened. Jutted against the fabric.

Holding her breath, she crossed her arms and grasped the hem of the nightdress, pulled it up and over her head. Wearing only a pair of pink panties, she met his eyes, her pulse racing, and hoped he could see what she was offering. Not just her body, but all of her. Everything she'd kept from him before. Everything she'd been so afraid to share with him.

He slowly got to his feet and cupped her face in his hands, his touch so gentle it was all she could do not to cry. "You've never looked more beautiful."

She'd had men tell her she was beautiful before, too many times to count. But she'd never believed it. Until now.

He skimmed his hands up her sides, over her ribs, as he kissed her. A soft, sweet kiss that warmed her heart and seemed to fill an emptiness inside her—an emptiness she'd felt ever since she'd left Aidan.

She didn't know if she'd ever be able to walk away from him again.

She kissed him back. Undressed him slowly, her hands stroking his taut skin, feeling the play of muscles in his arms. His chest. She trailed her fingers down his stomach and he inhaled sharply. But he didn't stop her from undoing his pants, or helping him slide them down so he could kick them off. And when he stood before her, all hard planes and sharp angles, she hooked her thumbs into the elastic waist of her underwear and shimmied out of them. Pushed him onto his back on her bed and straddled him.

And in the dimly lit room, the silence broken by an occasional sigh or moan, she did what she'd never allowed herself to do fully, without reservation or fears.

She loved him.

CHAPTER FIFTEEN

AIDAN SAT ON the edge of the bed and watched Yvonne sleep. Her hair was a jumbled blond mess against the pillow, her lips parted, her expression peaceful.

He shouldn't have spent the night. He should've gotten dressed and left her alone in bed after they'd made love the first time, but she'd collapsed on top of him, her body lax and warm and coated in a fine sheen of sweat. He'd stroked her hair, the long line of her back, and tucked her against his side, and they'd both fallen asleep.

And when he'd woken reaching for her, for a moment he'd thought he was back in his own bed, dreaming of her as he did so many nights. But it wasn't a dream. She curled into him and kissed him, her soft hands seeking as she caressed him. They'd made love again, this time at a frantic pace.

He hadn't wanted the night to end.

He scrubbed a hand through his hair, not taking his eyes from her face. But of course, it had to end. All things did. As someone who worked the land, he knew that better than anyone. The grapes that came to life in the spring, that grew thick and bountiful in the summer and gave their fruit in the fall harvest, turned dormant during the cold winter months.

Life was a cycle. There were always new beginnings, just as there were endings. People died. Marriages became broken, some so badly no repair was possible.

Being with Yvonne last night, making love with her, holding her like he used to made him realize two things: he still wanted her. Probably still even loved her.

But he had to walk away.

He had no control over himself or his feelings about her. And if a man didn't have control, didn't have his pride, he had nothing.

She scared the hell out of him.

She shifted and stretched an arm over head, the sheet sliding down to reveal the curve of her naked breast. He couldn't look away. She was so beautiful, so alluring in ways she didn't even realize.

"Good morning," she said in a sexy, sleepy voice that about tore apart every rationalization he had for not sliding back into bed with her. A small frown creased her forehead. "Do you have to be to work early?"

He forced himself to stand. "No."

She glanced at the digital clock by the bed, and smiled seductively. "Why don't you get undressed and come back to bed?"

He wanted to. So badly his body ached with it. "I can't."

She slowly pulled the sheet up to her chin. "Can't?" she asked quietly. "Or won't?"

"Both."

"I see." She sat up, dragging the sheet with her. "If you say last night was a mistake, I may have to hurt you."

"It wasn't a mistake." He tucked his hands into his pockets. "But I don't want you to think it meant more than what it did."

"Is that so?" she asked haughtily. But she couldn't quite pull it off, not wearing just a sheet, her hair a mess, her delicate skin pink with stubble burn from his kisses. "In other words, you don't want me to think last night changed anything between us."

"It didn't."

"Speak for yourself. It changed everything for me." Clutching the sheet, she looked him in the eye but when she spoke her voice was hesitant. "Aidan, I…" She exhaled softly, then rushed on, "I'm in love with you. I've never stopped loving you."

His heart kicked against his chest. God help him, hope shone in her eyes. He hardened his heart against it. "You never stopped loving me?" he asked. "And yet you still left me."

She blanched. "Don't," she ordered, her voice choked. "We can move forward. Things can be different."

"They could," he agreed. "If we want them to be. But I don't want that. I made the mistake of loving you once before, of trusting you. I won't make that same mistake twice."

Before he could change his mind, before his resolve

waned, he turned and walked away, though everything inside him screamed not to. That this was an even bigger mistake than when he'd let her go before.

He ground his teeth. No. He hadn't let her go. She'd left. What if he did give them a second chance? What if she ended up as unhappy as she'd been before? If she left him again, he didn't think he'd survive it.

He was passing the kitchen when she caught up with him. She stabbed her arms into the sleeves of her robe and tightened the belt.

"So that's it?" she asked, scurrying in front of him to block his escape. "You're not even willing to give us another chance?"

He looked over her head at the door, but other than physically moving her, he couldn't leave. And he couldn't move her. He didn't trust himself to touch her.

"Look," he said, "what happened last night was…" Just sex. But he couldn't force the lie out. "It was… great." He winced at how lame that sounded. How inadequate his words were. "It was amazing. You were amazing."

"Oh, my God," she said with a harsh laugh. "You sound like every sleazy one-night stand my parents warned me about."

He did. But he couldn't admit the truth. That he'd needed her last night.

His shoulders ached with tension and he rolled them back. "I'm sorry if I gave you the wrong impression about what last night meant. But nothing's changed between us."

Yvonne wrapped her arms around herself. "No matter what I do," she said, her voice hoarse, "it'll never be enough for you. You'll never forgive me for leaving you."

"There's nothing to forgive. You said it yourself—we just aren't meant to be."

"What if we want to make it work?" Her voice wobbled, and to his horror, her eyes filled with tears.

"Don't—"

"I love you, Aidan. You. The man you are now, standing in front of me. Do you love me?"

Damn it, he didn't want to hurt her. "Yvonne, I…"

"Answer me!" She straightened her arms, her hands clenched into fists at her sides. "Do you love me? Not the woman I was seven years ago, but the woman I am now."

He wanted to beg her not to let those tears shimmering in her eyes fall. To pull her into his arms and hold her, to make love to her, to pretend there was no past between them. No future to consider.

"I can't love you. I don't want to."

"I see," she said, nodding slowly, her eyes huge and wounded in her pale face. "Well, then, I guess you're right. There is no hope for us."

"I'm sorry," he repeated. The words were inadequate but they were all he had.

"Oh, please, don't apologize," she said coldly, despite

the way her lower lip quivered. "After all, this is what you wanted, wasn't it? A chance to be the one to walk away from me. To show you're in complete control of the situation."

"This isn't revenge."

"No, it's just you bowing to your stupid pride. Your fears." She stepped aside. "Well, I hope pride keeps you warm at night, and that it's worth giving me up."

He hesitated.

She pointed at the door. "This is my home for another week, and I'd like you to leave now." When he still didn't move, her lips curled. "What are you waiting for? Haven't you heard? What Yvonne Delisle wants, Yvonne Delisle gets."

He left.

He had to. Being there, being with her hadn't changed the past or the mistakes they'd both made. But it could change what happened next. A future with Yvonne was a frightening proposition. Unknown. Out of his control.

She was right. This was about his pride. Because when she walked away before, his pride had kept him going. He couldn't trust her, couldn't love her again because he wasn't strong enough to face her leaving again.

IT WAS THE MORNING of Diane and Senator Wallace's wedding, and Yvonne couldn't have asked for a better day. The sun shone brightly in a clear blue sky, warmed the crisp, clean air. It was a perfect day for new beginnings. For the happy couple, it was the start of their new life together, one Yvonne prayed would be happy and filled with good health.

For her, it was the beginning of her return to her old life. An end to her time at the Diamond Dust. To any hopes she may have harbored over the last week and a half that Aidan would change his mind about them.

He hadn't. He never would.

She knocked on the dressing room door. Mark had really come through for them, finishing the renovations of the carriage house, including the additions of the kitchen and bathrooms.

"Come in," Diane called.

Yvonne stepped inside. Aidan's mother sat at the antique dressing table in a full slip, applying mascara.

"Is there a problem?" Yvonne asked, doing a quick check of the room.

Everything seemed to be in order. Diane's dress, a silver chiffon with a V-neck and three rosettes at the Empire waist, hung on the back of the closet door. Her bouquet was in a box near to the sofa, her shoes on the floor beneath the dress. Yvonne had checked the mini fridge in the corner and knew it was stock with bottled water. The bridesmaids, Connie and Marsha, Senator Wallace's lovely daughter, along with flower girls Payton and Abby, were getting their pictures taken with the groomsmen. The chairs were set up, the caterers were busy in the kitchen, the bar was stocked with

Diamond Dust wine, and soon the guests would start to arrive.

So far, so good.

"Everything's fine," Diane said, putting the mascara away. "Stop worrying."

Brushing her hair off her forehead with the back of her hand, Yvonne smiled. "In this case, it's my job to worry."

"It's going to be a wonderful day, a perfect day, thanks to you."

Yvonne's eyes stung with tears. She fiercely blinked them back. God, what was the matter with her? Wasn't this what she'd wanted? Why she'd come back to the Diamond Dust? To prove to the people who hadn't accepted her how capable she was, how worthy?

"Did Aidan find you?" Diane asked, watching her in the mirror.

"Yes," Yvonne managed to say. "He caught up with me about an hour ago."

Caught her as she was coming out of the kitchen, to tell her how much he and his family appreciated all her hard work for them the past few weeks. How well she'd done her job. Then he'd handed her an envelope. A bonus for a job well done, he'd said, acting as if she meant nothing more to him than any other employee.

She wanted to rip the check into tiny pieces and shove those pieces up his nose. Instead, she'd smiled coolly, offered him a so-polite-it-almost-killed-her thank-you, then walked away, as if her heart wasn't breaking.

She was leaving in approximately twelve hours, had her car packed and ready to go, was more than eager to put this whole experience behind her after spending the past week trying to avoid him. And he'd given her a bonus.

The bastard.

"I'm glad you and your family are happy with my services," she told Diane.

"We are," the older woman said as she stood. She crossed to Yvonne, surprising her by taking her hands. "I'm just sorry things didn't work out how I'd planned." She watched her carefully. "How, I think, both of us would've liked them to have worked out."

Yvonne was afraid kind words and the slightest offering of comfort would make her crumble, when she needed all her strength just to get through the day. She squeezed Diane's hands, then stepped back and headed for the door. "I'm sorry, too."

AIDAN HAD NOTHING against weddings, but if there was any possible way he could skip out on this one without his mother skinning him alive, he would.

As the organ music played, he stood by her side at the door to the carriage house. Brady and Matt were both at the far end of the building next to Al. They all wore dark suits, while Connie and Al's daughter were in soft blue. Payton and Abby as flower girls wore white.

Aidan smiled down his mother. "You look beautiful."

She'd had two chemo treatments so far, and while they'd made her tired and sick to her stomach, she'd been more concerned with having a full head of hair for her wedding. But even though she had dark circles under her eyes, even though her face was pale and she was exhausted and nauseous, she was beautiful. She was alive.

"You ready?" Diane asked as the string quartet started a new tune.

"Shouldn't I be asking you that?"

"Oh, I'm more than ready." She smiled up at him. "It's a beautiful day," she said, repeating his father's favorite phrase.

Aidan patted her hand. "That it is." He kissed her cheek. "Be happy."

She nodded and they started walking down the make-shift aisle, but not before he caught the sheen of tears in her eyes. Aidan walked his mother to meet her soon-to-be new husband, before joining his brothers as the minister started to speak.

It had been a long week. A difficult one, with the side effects of the chemo taking hold. But today was a celebration. The carriage house was filled with Al and Diane's families and friends. Chairs had been set up in the large room so they could all witness the ceremony, and then immediately after, the crew Yvonne had hired would whisk the chairs away and replace them with tables, while the guests enjoyed appetizers on the new covered patio out back.

He had to admit Mark and his team had done a hell of a job with the renovations. Wide oak boards covered the floor and white lights hung from the rafters. The walls had been painted a soft yellow, the windows had been replaced.

Yvonne had somehow managed to pull off this wedding despite a crazy time limit and a bride battling cancer. But she'd done it.

And she'd done it while keeping her distance from him. When they did happen to run into each other, she was always cool, polite and professional. Like this morning, when he'd given her that bonus for a job well done.

He hated it. Hated having her so close and knowing he couldn't touch her. Couldn't just sit and talk with her as he wanted. He'd lost any rights where she was concerned. Had given them up.

While J.C. walked to the small podium for the first reading, he scanned the crowd. He recognized most of the people but there was one person missing, the one he desperately wanted to see.

And then there she was. Yvonne. She stepped into view at the back of the room. Her black dress accentuated her curves; her sexy, strappy shoes made her legs seem endless. She had on a headset, carried a clipboard in one hand, her phone in the other. Aidan shifted. Felt as if his shirt were strangling him. He tugged at the collar, ignoring the curious glance Matt gave him.

Aidan flashed back to another wedding, held in a church in Savannah. Yvonne's parents had wanted them to have the grandest wedding the city had seen in decades, but he hadn't cared if they exchanged vows in a church in front of five hundred people or alone on a beach. He'd just wanted her.

Wasn't that why you wanted me? You wanted this. The package.

He stretched his neck, but still felt as if he couldn't swallow. Couldn't draw a full breath.

Connie went up to read next, her voice filtering through his memories.

"Love is patient," she said in a clear, strong voice, her gaze landing on Matt. "Love is kind. Love does not envy."

They were the same words said at Aidan's wedding.

"Love does not boast. Love is not proud."

Sweat dampened the hair at the back of his neck. Love might not be proud, but he sure as hell had been. Too proud. So concerned about bruising his pride that he'd put it ahead of the only woman he'd ever loved.

"Love," Connie continued, "always trusts."

Across the room, he caught Yvonne's eyes.

God, she'd been right about so many things. He *had* wanted to be the one to leave. To be in control. All those years of trying to manage everyone and everything was his way of protecting himself. But he didn't need control. All he really needed was Yvonne.

He stepped toward her, but was stopped by Brady's hand on his arm. "What are you doing?" his brother asked under his breath.

Aidan shook him off, not caring that over a hundred people were going to witness him groveling. "I'm going to get my wife back."

YVONNE'S EYES WIDENED. What was Aidan doing? He wasn't...he wouldn't...

But as she watched, he started toward her, a determined expression on his face.

Oh, dear Lord.

Up at the podium, Connie frowned, but managed to finish her reading as Aidan made his way down the aisle. Yvonne forced herself to stand her ground.

"Go back up front," she whispered harshly when he reached her.

"I want to talk to you."

"Now?" She looked behind him, saw that the entire room was staring at them—including Diane and Al. "We can talk later."

"If I try to talk to you later, you'll find something to do or a way to avoid me."

True. So very, very true. "You're embarrassing me," she hissed.

"I need you."

"Don't…" She cleared her throat. "Don't do this. Not now. For God's sake, not here."

He grasped her upper arms. "I need you in my life, by my side, and I don't care who knows it. I. Need. You."

Afraid her head was going to explode, she pressed her hands above her ears. "Stop. You're ruining the ceremony."

He was ruining everything. She'd gotten through the past week by telling herself he'd been right. They never would've made it. Hadn't they failed once before? He had no right to do this to her now when she was prepared to leave him again.

"Sorry," he said. He turned and waved at his mother and Al. "Sorry," he called. "Carry on."

Then he tugged Yvonne toward the door. Oh, no, he didn't. She dug in her heels. "I'm not going anywhere with you."

His eyes glittered. "Want to bet?"

Before she knew it, he'd swept her up in her arms and carried her out the door and into the bright spring sunshine.

"I am going to kill you," she promised quite calmly, despite the turmoil going on inside of her.

"I deserve it," he said simply, his strides long, his voice not breathless in the least from hauling her around like a one hundred ten—okay, one hundred fifteen— pound sack of potatoes.

She didn't struggle. Was honestly too shocked to, and by the time she realized she should be struggling, she'd regained enough sense to know that if she did, he would probably drop her. And she'd suffered enough humiliation today.

He strode toward the grove of trees behind the carriage house, the place she'd suggested would make a lovely backdrop for outdoor weddings. She was glad he'd gone in this direction, as it, at least, granted them a semblance of privacy.

He carefully set her on her feet, his hands on her arms to help her regain her balance.

She smacked him away. "How *dare* you? Have you lost your mind? I am running that wedding you so unceremoniously carried me out of. I have people in there who are counting on me to make sure this day goes as smoothly as possible." Her voice rose as she began to pace, her heels sinking into the ground. "I have at least one prospective client who is considering the Diamond Dust for her own wedding next summer. I've worked myself ragged to make sure this day goes off without a hitch, and what do you do? You make a spectacle of me in front of a hundred guests." Breathing heavily, she slapped her hands on her hips. "Well? What do you have to say for yourself?"

He yanked her to him and kissed her.

And for a moment, she was lost in his arms. "Don't," she warned, pushing him away. "Just...don't."

"I'm sorry," he said urgently. "I'm sorry I embarrassed you. That wasn't my intent." He took her by the shoulders and forced her to face him. "But when I saw you standing there, I realized how wrong I was to let you go." His eyes searched hers. "I love you."

She jerked away from his touch. "That's not fair. You can't just decide all of a sudden that you love me. Not after the way you hurt me." She shook her head.

"Please, hear me out." He wiped his palms down the front of his dark suit pants. "I've made so many mistakes. I didn't see that I'd tried to make you be someone you weren't. But none of my mistakes could ever come close to my letting you go the first time. I'm not about to repeat that error now. I love you," he insisted. "I love how you look and how you talk. I love how hard you work and how you're addicted to that stupid phone of yours."

She lifted her chin. "It's not an addiction. It's a convenience."

He grinned, taking her breath away. "I love how you pretend you're not pissed when you really are." His tone turned husky. Intimate. "I love how you dance and how you make love. I love that you don't back down from anything or anyone."

She blinked and tears coursed down her face. She wiped them away. "It's too late."

He gripped her arms, pulled her onto her toes. "Don't say that. Please, don't say that. I love you." He shook her and she grabbed ahold of his shoulders. "I've never stopped loving you. I want to spend the rest of our lives together. Please don't leave me again," he said hoarsely. "I don't think I could survive."

Sobbing, she covered her mouth with one hand.

"I love you, too," she told him, laughter mixing with her tears. "I love you. I won't leave you. I won't ever leave you again."

And as her husband kissed her, Yvonne finally found where she belonged.

* * * * *

COMING NEXT MONTH

Available September 13, 2011

You can find more information on upcoming
Harlequin® titles, free excerpts and more at
www.HarlequinInsideRomance.com.

New York Times *and* USA TODAY *bestselling author*
Maya Banks presents a brand-new miniseries

PREGNANCY & PASSION

When four irresistible tycoons face
the consequences of temptation.

Book 1—*ENTICED BY HIS FORGOTTEN LOVER*

Available September 2011 from Harlequin® Desire®!

Rafael de Luca had been in bad situations before. A crowded ballroom could never make him sweat.

These people would never know that he had no memory of any of them.

He surveyed the party with grim tolerance, searching for the source of his unease.

At first his gaze flickered past her, but he yanked his attention back to a woman across the room. Her stare bored holes through him. Unflinching and steady, even when his eyes locked with hers.

Petite, even in heels, she had a creamy olive complexion. A wealth of inky-black curls cascaded over her shoulders and her eyes were equally dark.

She looked at him as if she'd already judged him and found him lacking. He'd never seen her before in his life. Or had he?

He cursed the gaping hole in his memory. He'd been diagnosed with selective amnesia after his accident four months ago. Which seemed like complete and utter bull. No one got amnesia except hysterical women in bad soap operas.

With a smile, he disengaged himself from the group

around him and made his way to the mystery woman.

She wasn't coy. She stared straight at him as he approached, her chin thrust upward in defiance.

"Excuse me, but have we met?" he asked in his smoothest voice.

His gaze moved over the generous swell of her breasts pushed up by the empire waist of her black cocktail dress.

When he glanced back up at her face, he saw fury in her eyes.

"Have we *met?*" Her voice was barely a whisper, but he felt each word like the crack of a whip.

Before he could process her response, she nailed him with a right hook. He stumbled back, holding his nose.

One of his guards stepped between Rafe and the woman, accidentally sending her to one knee. Her hand flew to the folds of her dress.

It was then, as she cupped her belly, that the realization hit him. She was pregnant.

Her eyes flashing, she turned and ran down the marble hallway.

Rafael ran after her. He burst from the hotel lobby, and saw two shoes sparkling in the moonlight, twinkling at him.

He blew out his breath in frustration and then shoved the pair of sparkly, ultrafeminine heels at his head of security.

"Find the woman who wore these shoes."

Will Rafael find his mystery woman?
Find out in Maya Banks's passionate new novel
ENTICED BY HIS FORGOTTEN LOVER
Available September 2011 from Harlequin® Desire®!

Love and family secrets collide in
a powerful new trilogy from

Linda Warren

the Hardin Boys

Blood is thicker than oil

Coming August 9, 2011.

The Texan's Secret

Before Chance Hardin can join his brothers in
their new oil business, he must reveal a secret
that could tear their family apart. And his
desire for family has never been stronger, all
because of beautiful Shay Dumont.
A woman with a secret of her own....

The Texan's Bride
(October 11, 2011)

The Texan's Christmas
(December 6, 2011)

www.Harlequin.com

HSR71723

Harlequin® *Romance*

**Discover small-town warmth and community spirit
in a brand-new trilogy from**

PATRICIA THAYER

*Where dreams
are stitched...patch
by patch!*

Coming August 9, 2011.

Little Cowgirl Needs a Mom

Warm-spirited quilt shop owner Jenny Collins promises to
help little Gracie finish the quilt her late mother started,
even if it means butting heads with Gracie's father,
grumpy but gorgeous rancher Evan Rafferty...

The Lonesome Rancher
(September 13, 2011)

Tall, Dark, Texas Ranger
(October 11, 2011)

Love Inspired

Everything Montana Brown *thought* she knew about love and marriage goes awry when her parents split up. Shaken, she heads to Mule Hollow, Texas, to take a chance on an old dream— being a cowgirl…while trying to resist the charms of a too-handsome cowboy. A wife isn't on rancher Luke Holden's wish list. But the Mule Hollow matchmakers are fixin' to lasso Luke and Montana together—with a little faith and love.

Her Rodeo Cowboy
by Debra Clopton

MULE HOLLOW
HOMECOMING

Available September wherever books are sold.

www.LoveInspiredBooks.com